The Cost of Forever

John H. Adams

DEDICATION

To my dearest Cindy, You have been my rock through my accident and all the ups and downs in life, always my unwavering supporter. Your love means the world to me, and I could never have completed this book without you by my side during this 12-year journey.

And to all my family and friends who have passed,
Your memories live on in my heart, and I know, in some way, you are reading your own copy of this book. This is for all of you.

CONTENTS

Chapter 1: Desert Roads

The highway stretched ahead like a ribbon of scorched earth, disappearing into the distant horizon where the sky bled into the land. Max's hands gripped the steering wheel of his old pickup truck tightly, his bare hands white-knuckled against the cracked leather. The desert highway stretched endlessly before him, shimmering in the heat like a mirage. He glanced at the busted clock on the dashboard, its red digits flashing 10:32—a problem he hadn't gotten around to fixing in years. Not that it mattered. Time had felt stuck for a long time anyway, his foot pressing just enough on the gas pedal to keep the truck crawling forward. The engine rumbled beneath him, steady but tired, just like he was. The heat from the midday sun radiated through the windshield, searing the desert landscape into his mind—a fitting backdrop for the emptiness inside him.

He hadn't noticed the sweat beading on his forehead until it dripped down the side of his face, mixing with the salty tears that had dried there hours ago. The duffel bag sat on the passenger seat, fat and heavy, filled with cash that didn't belong to him. But then again, did anything anymore?

Max glanced over at it, a dark shape covered by the faded plaid blanket he and Eve used to take on camping trips. Back then, when life was simpler, and the world felt open, full of promise, they'd sit around a fire beneath the stars, dreaming about their future. Eve would lay her head on his shoulder, eyes closed, whispering about the home, the family, and the life that they'd one day have. Those nights had felt like promises written in the stars.

But dreams turned into ghosts when you weren't looking. Some dreams died before they ever had the chance to breathe. They slipped away, invisible until the moment you realized you couldn't grasp them anymore. Now Eve was fading faster than those dreams ever had, and Max was left with this—an aching heart, a sickening weight of guilt in his chest, and stolen money in a duffel bag.

The desert outside was nothing but sand and rocks, a wasteland devoid of life. He supposed it wasn't too different from his own world now. His heart had long since turned to dust the day the doctor told them Eve had cancer. Terminal. The word still echoed in his mind like a death knell, a word that stole the air from his lungs and shattered everything he believed about fairness, about hope.

He pulled the truck over to the side of the road, letting the engine idle as he stared out into the distance. He knew he should keep driving, should get as far away as he could, but there was no escaping this—not really. It didn't matter where he went; he couldn't outrun the fact that he had failed her. Failed them both.

With a sigh, Max turned the engine off and leaned back in the seat, letting the silence close in around him. He closed his eyes, but all he could see was Eve—her pale face against the hospital pillow, the way her once vibrant eyes had dulled with pain and exhaustion. He could still hear her voice, soft and broken, as she tried to reassure him that it was okay, that she wasn't afraid to go. But she didn't know how much he was afraid of letting her go. How much he needed her to stay.

He'd done everything he could to save her—worked double shifts, took out loans, sold everything they owned of value. But it wasn't enough. It was never enough. The treatments had drained their bank account, and the doctors had drained their hope.

That's when the idea had taken root. He didn't even remember exactly when or how, but it grew inside him like a dark seed, fueled by desperation and a need to fix what was breaking. He told himself he could do it—just one job, one robbery. The bank in their small town was old, with a skeleton crew, nothing like the big city banks. He could get in, get the money, and get out before anyone even knew what happened.

He hadn't planned for Mr. Davis, the bank manager, to be there. He hadn't planned for the silent alarm. He hadn't planned for the police to arrive so fast.

The memory came back in flashes—the cold sweat on his skin, the hard gaze of Mr. Davis, the rising panic as the sirens wailed outside. And then the shot. God, that shot. The crack of the bullet had reverberated in his skull, louder than anything he'd ever heard. He didn't even know if the bullet had hit him, or if he was just…here now. Wherever here was.

Max blinked, bringing himself back to the present. The truck sat still, the engine silent, the world around him a scorching hell of rock and sand. And there, next to him, she appeared.

Eve.

He could see her in the corner of his eye, sitting in the passenger seat, where the duffel bag had been just moments ago. Her skin was pale, too pale, her hair thinner than he remembered, but her eyes—the soft brown eyes he had fallen in love with when they were just kids—were the same.

She smiled at him, a sad, knowing smile.

"You should've just let me go," she said quietly, her voice as soft as the wind brushing across the dunes.

Max swallowed hard, his throat tight. "I couldn't."
Her gaze drifted to the rearview mirror. "We can't go back now. You know that, right?"

Max nodded, feeling the weight of her words settle into the pit of his stomach. "I just wanted more time. I wasn't ready."

"No one ever is." She reached out, her hand hovering over his. "But you're still here."

Max felt a lump rise in his throat as he turned to look at her. "I don't know what to do anymore, Eve. I thought...I thought this would make it right."

Her fingers lightly brushed against his hand, though he could barely feel her touch. "You can't fix everything, Max. Sometimes you just have to let go."

He shook his head, his heart pounding. "Not you. I can't let go of you."

Eve's expression softened. "You never really lose the ones you love, Max. Not truly. But you can't keep holding on to something that's gone. It's time to let go."

Max turned back to the road ahead, his vision blurring with unshed tears. His voice cracked as he whispered, "I don't know how."

The wind outside picked up, swirling dust and sand across the road, obscuring the horizon. And when Max glanced back toward the passenger seat again, Eve was gone. The duffel bag sat where she had been just moments ago, heavy and silent, as though nothing had changed at all.

Chapter 2: Running from Ghosts

Max woke to the sound of gravel crunching beneath the tires of a passing car. His eyes snapped open, the midday sun stabbing at him through the windshield. He had fallen asleep, though he wasn't sure how long he'd been out. The truck was unbearably hot, the dry desert air pressing down on him like a suffocating blanket.

For a second, he thought he saw Eve again, her figure ghosting just beyond the haze of his vision, standing in the middle of the road. But when he blinked, she was gone, the mirage fading back into the desert heat.

The world around him felt like a furnace, the kind of heat that crawled under your skin and made every breath feel like an effort. The sun hung high in the sky, glaring down with an intensity that made the air itself shimmer. The inside of the truck had become a pressure cooker, the smell of hot leather and sweat clinging to everything. It reminded Max of the many summer days he had spent driving down backroads with Eve, the two of them laughing as they rolled the windows down and let the wind rush through their hair.

But now there was no laughter. No breeze to break the stifling heat. Just Max, alone, his pulse hammering in his temples, and the faint image of Eve lingering in his mind.

With a groan, Max rubbed his hands over his face and sat up straighter, wiping the sweat from his brow. He couldn't stay here. If the cops were looking for him—and he had no doubt they were—they'd find him sooner or later if he kept sitting on the side of the highway like this. Even in the middle of nowhere, there were eyes. There were always eyes.

He turned the key, and the truck sputtered back to life, the engine rumbling beneath his feet. The gas gauge hovered near empty, a dull reminder that his time was running out in more ways than one. He had enough to make it to the next town, maybe, but after that… he'd have to figure something out. And fast.

Max's hands gripped the steering wheel tighter as the truck rolled back onto the highway, the tires crunching over loose gravel before finding the smoother surface of the road. He couldn't shake the feeling of being watched, even though the road behind him had been empty for miles. His eyes flicked to the rearview mirror again—just to be sure. Nothing. Still nothing.

But that didn't make the paranoia any less real. In his mind, he could see the flashing blue lights, the squad cars racing down the highway behind him, gaining on him inch by inch. He could hear the sirens blaring in the distance, growing louder with every second. The bank. The blood. The echo of the gunshot still rang in his ears.

Mr. Davis. Max's jaw tightened at the thought of the bank manager. The old man's face had flashed through his mind a hundred times since he'd pulled the trigger—his wide eyes, the way his mouth had opened to protest, and then… nothing. Just the sound of the shot, the way the old man had crumpled to the ground. Max could still feel the weight of the gun in his hand, the cold metal biting into his palm.

The road ahead was a stretch of endless nothingness, but Max knew it led somewhere. It always did. Whether it was a diner with a broken neon sign or a gas station run by a guy who'd seen too much of the world and cared too little about anything, there was always something in the desert if you drove far enough.

The desert was like a void—vast and unforgiving. The longer Max drove, the more it felt like the road was swallowing him whole. The mountains in the distance were just jagged shadows against the sky, and the occasional tumbleweed that rolled across the road was the only sign of life. Even the desert seemed to be keeping its secrets, as if it knew the kind of man Max had become.

He'd heard stories about the desert—how it had a way of stripping a person down to their core, of forcing them to confront their demons. Maybe that's what was happening to him now. Maybe that's why he kept seeing Eve. The desert was reminding him of what he'd lost, of the promises he hadn't kept.

He pushed the truck into gear and eased it back onto the highway, his eyes scanning the rearview mirror. A habit, maybe, or just paranoia. Either way, the road behind him was as empty as the one ahead. No flashing lights, no sirens, just the whispering wind and the occasional buzz of a cicada breaking the silence.

His mind drifted, replaying the last few days in disjointed fragments. The plan had been simple: get in, get the money, and get out. A classic heist from an old movie script. Except this was real life, and in real life, nothing ever went to plan.

Max's pulse quickened as he remembered the moment before everything had gone wrong. The way the bank's cool air had hit him as he walked in, the duffel bag slung over his shoulder, his nerves rattling like a freight train in his chest. He hadn't planned on being noticed. He hadn't planned on being a killer. But in the heat of the moment, plans fell apart, and desperation took over.

He could still feel the eyes of the bank's customers on him, could hear the murmur of fear that had swept through the room as he'd pulled the gun from his waistband. He hadn't wanted to hurt anyone. He'd only needed the money. It was for Eve. It had always been for Eve.

He hadn't meant for anyone to get hurt. That part still gnawed at him, a constant ache in the pit of his stomach. The bank manager, Mr. Davis, had been an old man. Too old to be standing there, staring Max down like he was some kind of saint guarding the vault. And Max— sweating, heart pounding, the gun shaking in his hand— hadn't known what else to do. His finger had twitched. The shot had been loud. The blood, even louder.

Max gripped the wheel tighter, his hands aching under the pressure. It didn't matter how many times he tried to convince himself that he hadn't meant to do it. He had pulled the trigger. Mr. Davis was dead. And Max was a murderer now.

He hadn't come to terms with it yet. How could he? He wasn't the kind of man who killed in cold blood—at least, that's what he told himself. But every time he closed his eyes, he saw Mr. Davis's face. He saw the way the life had drained out of him, the way the blood had soaked into the floor of the bank. He saw the way the other customers had looked at him after that—like he wasn't even human anymore.

And now, sitting behind the wheel of his truck, miles away from the bank, from the town, from everything, Max couldn't escape the feeling that he was running. Not just from the law, but from himself.

But it had all been for her. For Eve.

And maybe, in some twisted way, that made it okay. Or at least it made it bearable.

The horizon wavered in the heat, and as the minutes ticked by, a structure finally appeared—a small, dusty gas station, barely more than a shack with a single pump. The kind of place you'd find in an old Western, with a lone cowboy waiting to duel at high noon. Only now, there were no cowboys, just Max and his empty gas tank.

As Max pulled up to the gas station, the truck's engine sputtered and groaned as if it was just as desperate for a break as he was. The gas gauge needle flirted with empty, barely hovering above the red line. The pump stood like a relic from a time long forgotten, weathered and beaten by the desert winds. Faded advertisements for motor oil clung to the station's walls, and an old, broken-down truck sat abandoned near the back of the lot, its rusted frame a stark reminder of things left to decay.

Max killed the engine and stepped out into the oppressive heat, the dry air instantly wrapping around him like a heavy blanket. The ground beneath him was cracked and dusty, the kind of place where it hadn't rained in years. His boots scuffed against the gravel as he made his way to the pump, glancing around as if expecting someone—anyone —to appear from behind the grimy windows of the small shop.

But there was no one. The station seemed as empty as the road behind him.

He grabbed the nozzle and jammed it into the truck's gas tank, letting the fuel flow as his mind wandered.

What now?

He had money in the duffel bag—plenty of it. More than enough to fill up the truck, to buy food, to keep driving until he was nothing but a forgotten ghost in the wind.

But was that the plan? To disappear?

"Not that simple," he muttered to himself, shaking his head. Running wouldn't solve anything. The weight of what he'd done would follow him no matter how far he drove. And Eve... Her voice lingered in the back of his mind, soft and sad. She had always been the good one, the one with the gentle smile and the kind eyes. The one who believed in second chances, in redemption.

He watched the numbers on the pump slowly climb, but it was as if time had stopped altogether. The rhythmic clicking of the gas filling the tank seemed too loud in the stillness, like the beat of a drum leading him toward something he didn't want to face. The desert stretched out around him, vast and indifferent, as if mocking the weight of the decisions he had made.

Max's thoughts drifted back to the moment in the bank, the moment when everything had gone wrong. He hadn't planned to shoot Mr. Davis. He hadn't planned to kill anyone. But the moment had spiraled out of his control, and now he was left standing in the middle of nowhere, pumping gas like nothing had changed.

Except everything had changed. Everything.

He replaced the nozzle and screwed the gas cap back on, then walked toward the small shop attached to the gas station. The bell above the door jingled as he stepped inside, and the cool air-conditioning hit him like a welcome shock. The inside was as rundown as he'd expected—faded posters for old beer brands plastered the walls, a rack of dusty snacks stood in one corner, and the man behind the counter looked like he hadn't seen a customer in days.

Max glanced around, taking in the dim interior. The faint hum of the air conditioner was the only sound, aside from the shuffle of the man's boots behind the counter. His graying beard looked like it hadn't been trimmed in months, and his sunken eyes gave the impression that he'd seen more than his share of hard times. The television behind him flickered with images of static, though Max doubted the old man was even paying attention to it.

Max grabbed a bottle of water and a bag of chips from a nearby shelf, the crinkling of the plastic cutting through the oppressive quiet. When he approached the counter, the man's gaze flicked up briefly before he reached out to grab the items without a word. His hands moved slowly, methodically, like someone who had spent years in the same routine without deviation.

Max tossed a few bills on the counter, but just as he was about to turn away, the man's voice cut through the silence.

"Where you headed?" the attendant asked, his tone casual but laced with something else. Curiosity? Suspicion?

Max paused, one hand on the door. His heart pounded in his chest, but he forced himself to keep his expression neutral. "Just passing through," he replied, his voice flat.

The man grunted, leaning slightly against the counter as he slid the money into the cash register. "Ain't much out there but more of the same," he said, his eyes narrowing ever so slightly as if he could sense there was more to Max's story than he was letting on.

Max nodded, his eyes narrowing slightly. "I'm used to it."

The man didn't say anything after that, just gave a slight shrug before turning his attention back to the small TV perched on a shelf behind the counter. The news was on, the volume low, but the images flickered across the screen —a bank, police cars, a stretcher being wheeled into an ambulance.

Max's stomach twisted, and his feet felt glued to the floor. He couldn't hear the words, but he didn't need to.

He knew what they were talking about. He knew the images all too well.

Max swallowed hard, a cold sweat breaking out on the back of his neck. His heart thudded in his chest as he stared at the screen for a moment longer, the memories from the bank rushing back in vivid detail. He could feel the weight of the gun in his hand, the way it had kicked when he'd pulled the trigger, the way Mr. Davis had crumpled to the floor, his blood pooling beneath him.

The gas station attendant's eyes flicked toward the screen, then back to Max. His expression hadn't changed, but there was something in his gaze that made Max's pulse quicken. Did the man recognize him? Was he piecing it together?

Max forced his legs to move, pushing through the door and back out into the blistering heat. The air outside felt thick and suffocating compared to the cool, stagnant air inside the station. He could feel the weight of the old man's gaze following him as he climbed into the driver's seat, the engine roaring to life beneath him.

As he pulled away from the gas station, the sky seemed to darken, a thin line of clouds creeping in from the horizon. The air felt heavier now, thick with the promise of a storm. Max glanced at the rearview mirror again, but this time, it wasn't just habit. It was fear. Fear that the past was catching up to him faster than he could run.

The wind picked up, howling across the desert as the first drops of rain began to splatter against the windshield. And through the storm, through the chaos, Max saw her again.

Eve.

She sat in the passenger seat, her eyes on the road ahead, her face pale but serene.

"You can't keep running forever," she said softly, her voice barely audible over the sound of the wind.

Max's heart pounded in his chest, his hands trembling on the wheel. "I'm not running," he lied, his voice tight.

But even as he said the words, he knew they weren't true.

He was running.

And there was nowhere left to hide

Chapter 3: Echoes on the Wind

The rain came down in sheets now, the sky an angry, swirling mass of dark clouds. The storm had come out of nowhere, like a vengeful god sent to chase him down, to wash away any trace of the man he used to be.

The rain wasn't just heavy—it was relentless, drumming against the roof of the truck like a thousand tiny fists. The windshield wipers swung back and forth in a losing battle, trying to keep up with the deluge. It was as if the storm itself was angry, determined to sweep him off the road and bury him in the desert.

Max's foot pressed harder on the gas pedal, the engine groaning in protest as the truck plowed through puddles forming on the cracked asphalt. Each time the tires hit water, the truck shuddered, threatening to skid, but Max barely flinched. He had driven through worse storms before, but none like this. None that seemed so… personal.

Eve's voice still echoed in his mind, the soft words playing on a loop, like a song he couldn't shake.

"You can't keep running forever."

She wasn't real, of course. At least, not in the way she used to be. But her presence was always there, just out of reach, a memory that refused to fade.

Every time he heard her voice, it was like a knife twisting in his chest. The guilt was suffocating, creeping up on him in the quiet moments—moments like this, when the world around him became nothing but the roar of the storm and the steady hum of the truck's engine.

"You can't keep running forever."

He wanted to scream back at her, to shout that he had no choice. Running was all he had left now. What was the alternative? To stop? To face the consequences of everything he had done? No. He wasn't ready for that. Not yet.

Max drove through the rain, the wipers struggling to keep up with the torrent of water that blurred the windshield. The road was slick, barely visible in the downpour, but he kept going. There was no turning back now. He had burned that bridge a long time ago.

His chest tightened as he leaned forward, his face just inches from the steering wheel, trying to make out the shape of the road ahead. The rain slashed at the glass like claws, turning the world into a murky, shifting blur. Max could feel the weight of his decisions pressing down on him, heavy as the storm clouds above.

His phone buzzed from the passenger seat, the screen lighting up with a message. He glanced at it, his heart skipping a beat.

Unknown Number: I know what you did.

For a moment, the world seemed to tilt beneath him. His chest tightened, and the air in the truck felt too thick to breathe. The storm outside seemed to close in, the walls of the cab growing smaller with every breath he took. He grabbed the phone, his fingers trembling as he swiped open the message. The words were simple, but the weight behind them was crushing.

Someone knew.

Someone was watching him.

The idea struck him harder than the rain. It felt like the storm was in his mind now too, swirling with thoughts he couldn't push away. He could feel eyes on him, tracking his every movement, waiting for him to slip up. Who could know? Who would send a message like this?

His pulse pounded in his ears, competing with the drumming rain. His heart raced in his chest, as if trying to escape the inevitable.

The phone buzzed again, another message from the same number.

Unknown Number: You can't run forever.

Max's hands shook as he dropped the phone back onto the seat. His mind raced, trying to make sense of it. Was it the police? Had they tracked him down? But the messages didn't feel like law enforcement—they felt personal. Someone was toying with him, playing a twisted game.

He pressed his foot harder on the gas, the truck lurching forward as the engine strained against the growing storm. The rain was relentless, hammering against the windshield, and the world outside the truck was a blur of gray and shadow. Max could barely see the road ahead, but he didn't care. He needed to get away, to outrun whatever was closing in on him.

The truck lurched as it hit a patch of standing water, the tires slipping for a heart-stopping second before catching traction again. Max's hands straining as he gripped the steering wheel, his breaths coming in shallow, ragged gasps. His heart pounded in his chest like a drumbeat, faster and faster with every passing second.

The phone buzzed again. He didn't look this time. He couldn't.

As the storm raged around him, Max's mind spiraled, flashes of the past colliding with the present. He saw Eve's smile, the way her eyes crinkled at the corners when she laughed. He remembered the nights they spent dreaming about a future that never came. And he remembered the way her face looked the last time he saw her—pale, distant, as if she had already slipped away from him before he ever realized it.

He had done everything for her. Every desperate move, every broken promise, every crime. It was all for Eve. But now, as he sped down this desolate road in the middle of a storm, he couldn't help but wonder if she had ever asked for any of it. If she had ever wanted him to go this far.

Max wiped at his eyes, but it wasn't just the rain that blurred his vision.

Suddenly, headlights cut through the darkness behind him. Bright. Blinding. They appeared out of nowhere, closing in fast.

Max's heart pounded in his chest, adrenaline spiking through his veins. The headlights swerved, matching his every move, the vehicle behind him weaving dangerously close. Panic clawed at him as he slammed the gas pedal to the floor, the truck fishtailing on the slick road.

The headlights stayed with him, closer now. Too close.

Whoever it was, they weren't just following him—they were hunting him.

Max's pulse raced as he glanced at the rearview mirror, his breath coming in shallow bursts. He could see the outline of the vehicle now, a dark SUV, its grille snarling through the rain like a predator stalking its prey. His mind scrambled for answers—who was it? The police? Someone else?

He didn't have time to figure it out.

Up ahead, the road twisted sharply to the left, curving along the edge of a steep ravine. The rain had turned the dirt into mud, slick and treacherous. Max's truck skidded as he took the turn too fast, the back end fishtailing wildly. For a moment, he thought he'd lost control, but the tires caught just enough traction to keep him on the road.

The SUV behind him wasn't as lucky.

Max watched through the mirror as the headlights veered sharply to the side, the vehicle sliding off the road and plunging into the ravine. There was a sickening crunch as metal met rock, and then the headlights were gone, swallowed by the darkness.

Max's chest heaved, his hands still gripping the wheel as the adrenaline coursed through him. He had escaped. For now.

But as he drove on, his heart still hammering in his chest, he couldn't shake the feeling that it wasn't over. Whoever had sent the messages… they weren't done with him. This wasn't just a chase. It was a warning.

He was being hunted.

Chapter 4: The Stranger on the Road

Max drove for what felt like hours, the rain easing into a steady drizzle, though the air still crackled with the remnants of the storm. The adrenaline that had surged through his veins after the SUV plunged into the ravine was wearing off, leaving him feeling hollow and raw. Every muscle ached from the tension of constant fear, and his hands throbbed, holding so tight to the steering wheel.

The road went on like a dark ribbon cutting through the barren desert. The silhouettes of jagged rocks loomed in the distance, barely visible under the thin veil of moonlight that broke through the shifting clouds. A strange stillness settled over the landscape, as though the world itself had paused. But Max couldn't shake the feeling that something was out there—something unseen but closing in. The air itself seemed heavier, the quiet too perfect, pressing against his chest like the weight of an unseen watcher.

He glanced at his phone, half-expecting another message from the unknown number. The screen remained dark, but the last words were seared into his mind.

"You can't run forever."

The words clung to him like the dampness of the air, no matter how hard he tried to push them aside. Max knew he had enemies, but this felt different. It wasn't revenge, nor was it just about the money. No, this felt… personal, as though someone knew him—knew everything.

The truck's engine hummed beneath him, the low, steady vibration offering little comfort. He had been running for so long now, from everything and everyone, that stopping seemed alien to him. What did it even mean to stop? To face the consequences? The idea felt foreign, almost impossible. All he knew was the road ahead, stretching endlessly, and the weight in his chest telling him to keep going.

As he rounded a bend, something flickered in the distance —a figure walking along the shoulder of the road. Max squinted, his heart giving a slight jolt. The man was tall, his dark coat clinging to him as the rain misted around him. He walked slowly, deliberately, as if he had been walking for miles and had nowhere left to go. For a moment, Max thought the figure blurred into the dark landscape, like a trick of the eyes.

The headlights hit him, and Max blinked. He was there, wasn't he? The figure appeared again, solid this time.

Max's grip tightened on the wheel as an odd chill crept up his spine, colder than the drizzle against the windows.

The silhouette seemed to materialize from the mist, as though it had been there all along, unnoticed until now. The figure moved slowly, hunched slightly, his coat whipping in the breeze like something caught between two worlds. The man didn't wave, didn't react to the piercing beams of Max's headlights. He simply kept walking, his pace steady, his presence unnerving, like a ghost that didn't belong on this stretch of highway.

Max's first instinct was to keep driving, to let this stranger remain a shadow in the distance. He didn't need to stop— not now, not with everything closing in. But something made him pause. Maybe it was the eerie stillness, the strange sensation that the world itself had frozen for a moment. Maybe it was the way the man moved— unnatural yet familiar—or maybe it was the crushing weight of guilt twisting deep in Max's gut. Whatever it was, Max hesitated.

The air inside the truck felt thicker, heavier somehow, as though the presence of the figure had changed something, but Max couldn't quite put his finger on it. His chest tightened with the weight of it, but he pushed it down. After all, what difference could it make now?

Against his better judgment, Max slowed the truck and rolled down the window, the cold air slipping inside like a creeping whisper.

"Need a lift?" Max's voice felt rough, scraped raw by the tension coiled in his chest.

The man turned slowly, his face hidden beneath the shadow of his hood. For a heartbeat, the world seemed to still. The rain tapped against the roof, but even that sound felt muted. Somewhere in the distance, thunder rolled, but the stranger stood silent. The moment stretched unnervingly, as if Max had called out into a void. Then, with deliberate, unhurried movements, the man nodded and climbed into the passenger seat.

For a moment, Max could have sworn the temperature in the truck dropped, though the engine still hummed and the vents blew warm air. The stranger settled in, not saying a word, and Max noticed a faint, earthy smell—like rain-soaked dirt—that filled the cab.

The door creaked, the sound unnaturally loud in the silence that settled between them as the man sank into the seat beside Max. The faint scent of damp earth and rain filled the cab, clinging to the stranger's coat as if it had soaked into him. Max glanced at him from the corner of his eye as they began to drive, the road stretching endlessly into the night. The stranger didn't seem to mind the quiet —if anything, he welcomed it. His hands rested calmly on his knees, his posture too still, his eyes fixed ahead as if the road held no secrets, no destination, just the present moment.

Max felt the tension simmering beneath the surface, an inexplicable pressure, as though the presence of this man had changed the air in the truck. It wasn't anything Max could define, but it was there—a sense that something was off, something he couldn't quite name.

A few miles passed before Max finally broke the silence, the weight of it pressing against his chest.

"You got a name?"

The stranger turned his head slowly, just enough for Max to catch a glimpse of his face. His features were sharp— hard jawline, a shadow of stubble—but it was his eyes that caught Max's attention. They seemed older than the man himself, calculating and cold, as if they had seen too much. A chill prickled the back of Max's neck.

"Eli," he said, his voice low, almost too soft to hear over the hum of the engine.

Max waited for more, but Eli offered nothing else. Just his name. Max had met men like Eli before—the kind who kept their thoughts locked away, who didn't trust easily, if at all. Yet there was something about Eli that felt different, as though he wasn't just withholding information, but existing on a different plane entirely. The silence stretched between them again, but this time, it felt heavier, as if the air in the cab had thickened.

The silence between them lingered, thick with the weight of words left unsaid. The truck's engine hummed softly beneath them, the sound blending with the tires crunching over wet asphalt. Yet the tension in the cab felt palpable. Max couldn't shake the feeling that something was off—not just with the man beside him, but with everything. Where had Eli come from? And why did his presence feel like a shadow creeping into the corners of Max's mind?

His thoughts circled back, over and over, gnawing at him like an itch he couldn't scratch. He stole another glance at Eli, catching the way the man stared blankly ahead, his expression unreadable. The air seemed colder inside the truck, despite the steady warmth blowing from the vents.

"What brings you out here?" Max finally asked, forcing casualness into his tone, though his gut twisted with unease.

Eli didn't answer right away. He just shrugged, the movement slow, deliberate. "Same thing as you, I reckon."

Max's grip on the steering wheel tightened, his fingers turning white. "And what's that?"

Eli's gaze flicked toward him for a brief moment, a flicker of something unreadable in his eyes before he looked away again. "Running," he said, the word hanging in the air like a shadow. The tone in his voice was strange—like it carried more weight than just a simple answer. Like Eli knew exactly what Max was running from, even if Max wasn't ready to admit it.

Max's heart gave an uncomfortable lurch. He opened his mouth to speak but found himself hesitating, the words caught in his throat.

The word hit Max like a punch, knocking the air from his lungs. His mind raced, thoughts tumbling over each other.

How much did this guy know? Was it just a coincidence, or had Eli somehow been waiting for him all along?

"You don't know anything about me," Max muttered, his voice low, a growl creeping into his tone as he tried to keep control.

Eli turned his head slowly, and for the first time, Max caught a glimpse of a faint smile playing at the corners of his lips—a smile that didn't quite reach his eyes. "You're right. I don't," Eli said softly, the words almost too smooth, too casual. "But I know the look. The way you drive, the way you watch the road like you're expecting something—like you're waiting for something to catch up to you. It's a familiar story."

The words slid through the cab like a chill wind. Max's skin prickled, and his heart thudded unevenly in his chest. He kept his eyes trained on the road, but the air felt different—heavier, colder. Eli had hit too close to the truth, and the way he sat there, so calm, so certain, made Max's stomach churn. There was something unnatural in the way Eli observed him, as though the man already knew everything Max was hiding.

The wind outside picked up, rustling the trees, the branches scraping together like brittle bones. Inside the cab, the silence grew heavier, as if the world around them had paused. Max's thoughts spiraled, each one darker than the last. Every moment of quiet between them seemed to add another layer of tension, thick and suffocating. There was something about Eli—something dangerous, lurking just beneath the surface. But Max couldn't put his finger on it.

It wasn't just what Eli said—it was how he sat, so composed, so certain, as if he knew things he shouldn't. Max's unease deepened with each passing minute, the small inconsistencies gnawing at him. The man felt too familiar, and yet too strange at the same time. Like something wasn't quite right, like a shadow that never quite matched the shape it cast.

They drove in silence for what felt like miles, the road stretching endlessly before them. The weight in Max's chest pressed harder. Finally, Eli's voice cut through the quiet, startling Max from his thoughts.

"You hear about the accident back there?"

Max's stomach clenched, a cold wave of dread washing over him, but he forced his expression to stay impassive. "What accident?"

Eli didn't look at him, his gaze still fixed ahead. "Big SUV. Slid off the road, down into a ravine. Cops'll probably find it by morning, if they haven't already."

Max squeezed the steering wheel, his knuckles pulsing. "That so?" His voice felt strained, and he couldn't shake the feeling that Eli knew more than he was letting on—more than he should know. The way he spoke, so casual, made the hairs on Max's arms stand up.

Eli nodded, his eyes narrowing ever so slightly as he turned his gaze toward Max. "Funny thing, though. When they found it—there was no one in the driver's seat. Doors were wide open. But the driver… gone."

Max's breath caught in his throat, his heart thudding painfully in his chest. How did Eli know that? The way he said it, as if he had been there, watching, made Max's skin crawl. He swallowed hard, his throat dry. He didn't know how much Eli knew or how he could possibly know it, but it was becoming clear that Eli wasn't just some random hitchhiker.

A strange pressure filled the cab, as though the very walls were closing in around them. The air felt heavier, almost suffocating, as Eli's words sank deeper into Max's mind. The memory of the SUV crashing into the ravine flickered like a dark, unsettling vision. Max had barely escaped that night, the sound of metal on rock echoing in his ears. But Eli's calm, unnervingly composed demeanor only made Max's unease grow.

Max glanced at him, trying to keep his voice steady, but the cold edge in it was impossible to hide. "What do you want?"

Eli leaned back, his eyes never leaving Max, as if he were reading him, peeling back layers Max didn't even know were there. "Same thing you want," Eli said softly, his voice a smooth, unhurried drawl. "To survive. And right now, it looks like we're both running from the same problem."

Max's pulse quickened, the steady thrum of it echoing in his ears. "What problem?"

Eli's smile widened slightly, but it didn't reach his eyes. Those eyes—dark, calculating—held something cold, something far removed from the light grin on his lips. "Whoever's after you," Eli said, his voice dipping lower, more ominous, "they're after me too."

Max's mind raced. Was this some kind of trap? Had Eli been waiting for him, guiding him here all along? He couldn't shake the suspicion, the gnawing sense that none of this was as simple as it seemed. But the calm certainty in Eli's voice—the absolute confidence with which he spoke—made Max's skin crawl.

"I don't know what you're talking about," Max muttered, though even as the words left his mouth, they felt hollow, a flimsy defense against a truth he wasn't ready to face.

Eli chuckled, the sound low and dark, like a distant storm brewing on the horizon. "You will."

The words hung in the air between them, thick with something unspoken, something that chilled Max to the core. For the briefest moment, Max could have sworn the lights in the truck flickered, just for a heartbeat, and then everything was still again—unnaturally still.

Max's phone buzzed again, lighting up on the dashboard.

He didn't need to look to know what it said.

Chapter 5: Whispers of the Past

The sky darkened quickly, storm clouds rolling in like heavy curtains, swallowing the last traces of daylight. Max tightened his grip on the steering wheel, his hands blanching with the strain. Every mile felt longer than the last, every road sign pointing toward nothing. Beside him, Eli sat in silence, his gaze fixed ahead, too still. There was a strange calm about him, a serenity that gnawed at Max's nerves more than the storm gathering above them.

The truck's engine droned steadily, its hum filling the cab, but it did little to ease the tension in Max's chest. It had been building since the moment Eli climbed in, tightening with every word, every glance. The air outside grew thick with moisture, and the weight of it seemed to seep into the truck, pressing down on Max's lungs with each breath. The sky churned, but Eli remained unmoved, untouched by the growing storm.

Max shot a glance toward Eli, unable to shake the unnerving sense of wrongness that had settled between them. How could someone be so calm after everything that had happened? The man's unflinching demeanor only added to the strangeness that surrounded him. Max's mind raced, replaying their brief conversations, searching for answers that eluded him. He shook his head, trying to push the thoughts aside. He needed to focus—get to the cabin, lay low, and figure out what the hell was going on.

But there it was again—the feeling that something wasn't right, that Eli was more than he seemed. The sky outside darkened, but it wasn't just the storm—it was something else, something that made the edges of Max's vision blur, made the air in the cab feel colder than it should have been.

The rain started as a light drizzle, the kind that barely tapped the windshield. But within minutes, it escalated, coming down in torrents, hammering the glass with relentless force. The windshield wipers struggled, swinging back and forth in a futile attempt to keep up. Ahead, the road blurred into streaks of black and gray, as if the storm had swallowed it whole. The rain wasn't just heavy—it was fierce, almost purposeful, as though it knew exactly where Max was headed and wanted to stop him.

The wind howled through the cracks in the doors, making the truck shudder as it sped down the slick road. But through it all, Eli remained motionless, staring ahead as if the storm were nothing more than background noise, his calmness an unsettling contrast to the chaos swirling outside.

"I think we should pull over," Eli said suddenly, his voice cutting through the roar of the storm like a blade. He didn't sound worried or frantic—just steady, unnervingly steady.

Max glanced at him, his frown deepening. "Pull over? Out here? Are you crazy?"

Eli turned his gaze toward Max, and for a split second, the air in the truck seemed to freeze. A cold chill snaked down Max's spine, prickling at the base of his neck. Eli's calm demeanor, in the face of the storm raging around them, was more than just unsettling—it was unnatural. "There's something coming," Eli said, his voice low, but firm, like a truth that had already been written. "You can't outrun it."

Max's heart hammered in his chest, his pulse quickening. He didn't know what it was—whether it was the storm outside, the tension that had been building since the job went wrong, or something else entirely—but Eli's words sent a shiver of dread curling through him. "What are you talking about?" Max muttered, his voice tight with confusion.

Eli didn't respond. He turned his head slowly, gazing out the passenger window, his reflection a faint, blurred silhouette through the rain streaking the glass. The truck's tires skidded slightly as they hit a patch of water, and Max cursed under his breath, tightening his grip on the wheel. He stole another glance at Eli, but the man remained completely unfazed, as though the storm's growing fury meant nothing to him.

The rain hammered the windshield, the wind howling like a living thing, but Eli sat in perfect calm. Max's pulse raced, an uneasy knot twisting tighter in his gut.

The road ahead twisted sharply, but Max barely registered it in time. He jerked the wheel, and the truck skidded dangerously close to the edge of the road, the tires catching on the muddy shoulder. For a moment, the world seemed to slow, the truck teetering on the brink, suspended between control and chaos. Max's heart lurched, and with a sharp pull, he wrenched the wheel, forcing the truck back onto the road.

He exhaled sharply, his pulse thundering in his ears, adrenaline coursing through him. But when he glanced at Eli, the man hadn't moved, hadn't flinched. Eli just sat there, calm as ever, his posture unchanged, his eyes still fixed ahead, as though the near-accident hadn't even happened. Max's skin crawled at the eerie stillness that radiated from him.

It wasn't natural. Nothing about Eli felt natural.

Max's hands trembled on the wheel as he muttered under his breath, "You knew that was coming, didn't you? What the hell are you?"

Eli turned his head slowly, his eyes locking onto Max with a gaze that felt unnaturally heavy. There was something in those eyes—something ancient, a knowing that seemed far older than the man beside him. Max could feel the weight of Eli's gaze pressing down on him, as if Eli could see through him, past the walls Max had built, right into the heart of his fear and guilt.

"I'm just here to help," Eli said, his voice calm, almost soothing. "But you're not listening."

Max's pulse quickened. Those words—so simple, yet so unnerving—echoed in his mind. He didn't know why, but something told him Eli wasn't just talking about the road ahead. He wasn't just talking about the storm. There was more, something Max couldn't quite grasp but felt on the edges of his thoughts, gnawing at him. He didn't react the way a normal person should. Didn't act like a man who had just gone through a bank robbery and a high-speed escape.

Max glanced in the rearview mirror. The road behind them was empty, but something in the distance tugged at his attention. A flash of light, a shadow darting across the horizon. He blinked, and it was gone.

"You need to pull over," Eli said again, his voice firmer now, though still calm.

Max felt the weight of Eli's words pressing down on him. His instincts screamed to keep driving, to get to the cabin, but something inside him, some primal part, made him ease off the gas. He slowed the truck, his eyes darting between the road and Eli. "Why? What's out there?"

Eli didn't answer right away. His gaze drifted toward the windshield, watching the rain blur the world outside. "Sometimes, it's not about what's out there," he said quietly. "It's about what's catching up to you."

Max's hands tightened again on the wheel, his jaw clenching. He didn't like where this was going. He didn't like the feeling that was creeping up his spine, the way Eli seemed to know more than he was letting on. But something in the man's words gnawed at him. It wasn't the storm or the threat of police catching up to them—it was something else, something deeper.

The truck hummed as Max pulled it to the side of the road, the tires sinking slightly into the mud. The rain poured down harder now, drumming against the roof of the truck like a thousand tiny hammers. Max killed the engine, and for a moment, the world outside seemed muted, the only sound the steady tap-tap of rain on metal.

Inside the cab, the air felt thick with tension, the silence pressing in around them. Eli shifted in his seat, turning to face Max fully. His face was shadowed by the dim light filtering through the rain-spattered windows, but his eyes gleamed with something Max couldn't place. "You can't keep running."

Max swallowed hard. "Running from what?"

Eli's eyes darkened, and for a brief moment, Max swore he saw something shift in the man's face—a flicker of something not quite human. The truck felt smaller now, the walls of the cab closing in as Eli's gaze bore into him. "From yourself."

The words hung in the air like a curse, and Max felt the full weight of them settle over him. He stared at Eli, his mind racing, trying to piece together what the hell was happening. Was this guy real? Was any of this real?

"You don't have to do this alone," Eli added, his voice softer now. "But you can't keep pretending it's all going to go away."

Max's breath caught in his throat. His mind reeled, searching for answers, but all he found was a growing sense of unease. Something about this—about Eli, about the storm, about the road ahead—felt wrong. Like a dream he couldn't wake up from.

Outside, the rain continued to pour, and the wind howled through the trees. But inside the truck, everything felt still. Too still.

Max turned away from Eli, his eyes scanning the road ahead. He couldn't shake the feeling that they weren't alone, that something—someone—was watching. Waiting.

"What do you want from me?" Max asked, his voice barely above a whisper.

Eli didn't answer. He just stared at Max, his eyes filled with a quiet intensity that chilled him to the bone.

And then, in the distance, through the blur of rain and darkness, Max saw it—a figure, standing in the middle of the road.

For a split second, he couldn't believe what he was seeing. The figure was cloaked in shadow, unmoving, as if it had been waiting for him all along. Max's heart raced, his mind struggling to make sense of the surreal scene. He blinked, and when his eyes refocused, the figure was gone.

Max shifted in his seat, his body tense, his mind spinning. The truck's engine hummed softly, the distant sounds of sirens a low, throbbing reminder of the chaos waiting for him outside. Eli leaned closer, his voice dropping to a conspiratorial whisper. "You know, sometimes you have to lose everything to find what truly matters."

Max shot him a sidelong glance, curiosity and unease mingling in his chest. "What do you mean?"

Eli paused, his gaze drifting to the window as if watching something only he could see. "You've made choices, Max. Some good, some… well, let's just say they could have been better." He smiled, but it didn't reach his eyes.

The moment hung heavy between them, and Max felt a wave of nostalgia wash over him. He thought of a classroom—bright, sunlight streaming through tall windows, laughter echoing off the walls. He was a boy then, filled with dreams and aspirations that felt so tangible. But that was another life, long buried beneath regrets and failures.

"Listen," Max said, shaking his head as if to clear the fog of memories. "I didn't come here for a life lesson."

"Maybe not. But isn't it time you faced your choices?" Eli's tone shifted, becoming sharper, more insistent.

Max turned to him, a flicker of defiance igniting within. "What do you know about my choices?"

"More than you think." Eli leaned back, the shadows of the truck cabin hiding his expression. "You're not the only one with something to lose."

Max swallowed hard, the tension in the air thickening. "And what's that supposed to mean?"

"Just… be careful," Eli said, his tone oddly gentle, almost protective. "You're in deeper than you realize."

As they sat in the growing silence, the weight of unspoken truths pressed down on them. Max couldn't shake the feeling that Eli was more than just a companion in this precarious situation. He was a mirror reflecting the darkness Max had tried to ignore.

Then, out of nowhere, a flash—a memory flared in his mind, sharp and vivid.

A classroom. Max sat at a desk, the smell of chalk dust filling the air. A young girl with braided hair, bright eyes, and an infectious smile stood in front of him, her laughter like a melody. He could hear the teacher's voice droning on, but all he could focus on was her. She'd spoken his name, her voice light and teasing, and he felt a warmth spread through him—a feeling of belonging, of hope.

"You can be anything you want, Max. Just believe in yourself," she had said, her confidence shining like a beacon.

He had nodded, enraptured, dreams swirling in his mind like colorful kites against a clear blue sky. But then the scene began to dissolve, fading into the shadows of his memory, the laughter replaced by the haunting silence of the present.

"Max? You okay?" Eli's voice broke through, and he snapped back to reality, heart pounding.

"Yeah, just… thinking," he muttered, trying to shake off the heaviness that clung to him. Eli nodded, his expression unreadable. "Just remember—whatever you think you're fighting for, it may not be what you truly want."

Max clenched his jaw, uncertainty gnawing at him. Outside, the world was unraveling, but in this moment, with Eli's enigmatic presence beside him, he felt caught between the past and the future—a collision of choices that would lead him down an uncertain path.

As the sirens wailed closer, Max knew he had to make a decision. With the weight of Eli's words pressing down on him, he understood that the battle wasn't just outside; it was within himself.

And for the first time, he wondered if the fight was worth the cost.

Chapter 6: The Weight of Silence

The road stretched ahead, darker now as the sun's dying light faded completely behind the hills. Max drove in silence, his mind a whirlpool of conflicting thoughts, each one louder than the hum of the truck's engine. The darkness outside seemed to press against the windows, as though the night itself was closing in on him.

The quiet was heavy, as if the world had drawn a thick curtain over them, leaving only Max and Eli in their small bubble of isolation. Eli sat beside him, silent as always, but his presence filled the space between them like a weight Max couldn't shake. There was something about him, something in the way he sat, almost too still, that set Max on edge. It reminded him of himself—how he'd sit on the edge of the hospital bed, waiting for the news that never came. And yet, it was more than that. The stillness felt familiar in another way, like looking at a shadow of something he should recognize, but couldn't place. He felt it in his gut, gnawing at him, like some part of him knew this person, or should have known him. Or maybe it was that Eli seemed to know things he shouldn't. Things about Max. Things about Eve.

The hum of the truck's tires against the road was rhythmic, almost soothing, but Max found no comfort in it. His thoughts were a jumbled mess, a constant cycle of regret and uncertainty. The rain had left the pavement slick and shiny, reflecting the faint glow of the headlights, but even that seemed distant now. He felt as though he were drifting, untethered, lost in the sea of his own memories.

Max's hold on the steering wheel tightened even more as the memories came rushing back. Eve's smile, her laughter. The way her eyes used to light up when they talked about the future. And then... the hospital. The doctors. The endless string of tests and the inevitable diagnosis that shattered everything.

He swallowed hard, forcing himself to focus on the road, but the past was relentless, clawing at the corners of his mind. It was always there, waiting for him in the quiet moments, ready to pull him under. He thought of the classroom again—the way Eve had been his anchor, even when they were kids. Her confidence, her strength. It was always Eve who believed they could rise above everything. Max had never been that sure.

"Do you ever think about what might have been?" Eli's voice broke the silence, soft but piercing, like he had reached into Max's thoughts and pulled the words straight from his mind.

Max didn't answer right away. The question lingered, hanging heavy between them.

"Of course I do," Max said finally, his voice rough. "But it doesn't change anything."

Eli nodded, looking out the window as if he could see beyond the darkness. The black of the night stretched on, endless and oppressive. The distant horizon was barely distinguishable from the sky, both blending into one impenetrable void. "No, it doesn't. But sometimes, thinking about it helps you see what you've been running from."

Max shot him a glance, suspicion threading through his mind. "You keep saying that. 'Running.' What do you think I'm running from?"

Eli smiled, that same eerie calm spreading across his face. "You know."

Max exhaled sharply, his frustration bubbling up. He didn't like how Eli could get under his skin so easily, with so few words. "No. You don't know anything about me."

Eli didn't respond right away. Instead, he reached into his coat pocket and pulled out something small, holding it up to the dim light in the truck. Max's breath caught in his throat when he saw it. A small, wooden figure. A tiny, handcrafted dollhouse chair, the kind Max used to make in his father's wood shop.

Max felt a chill crawl up his spine. "Where did you get that?"

Eli turned the chair over in his fingers, studying it like it was the most natural thing in the world. "I found it. Back there." His eyes flicked to the rearview mirror. "In the past."

Max swallowed hard, his pulse quickening. His mind raced back to the wood shop, to the afternoons he spent with his father building small things for Eve—like the dollhouse, a gift he'd given her when they were barely teenagers. It had been a symbol of their shared dreams, of the future they thought they could build together.

"Eve loved it," Max muttered, more to himself than to Eli. "She said it was the most beautiful thing anyone had ever made for her."

Eli nodded, his expression thoughtful. "Because it wasn't just wood and nails. It was hope. It was your promise to her."

Max felt a lump form in his throat. He hadn't thought about that in years. Not since everything had gone so wrong. He glanced at Eli, the unease growing inside him. "How do you know about that?"

Eli's eyes darkened, a shadow passing over his face. "I told you. I know more than you think."

Max wanted to press him, to demand answers, but something about Eli's tone stopped him. Instead, he turned his focus back to the road, the weight of his memories pressing down on him like a heavy stone.

The truck's engine hummed along, the rhythm of the tires on the road steady, yet there was nothing steady inside Max. His mind was swirling, not only with the past but with the present—the unease that Eli brought with him, the sense that there was something just out of reach, something he couldn't quite grasp.

They drove on in silence, the night closing in around them like a shroud. Max's thoughts drifted back to the hospital, to Eve lying in that sterile room, her body fragile, her breath shallow. He had done everything he could to save her. He had sacrificed everything. But in the end, it hadn't been enough.

"It's not your fault," Eli said suddenly, his voice cutting through the darkness.

Max blinked, startled. "What?"

Eli turned to face him, his expression serious. "It wasn't your fault. What happened to Eve. You couldn't have stopped it."

Max clenched his jaw, his hands tightening on the steering wheel. "You don't know that."

"I do," Eli said quietly. "Sometimes, no matter how hard we try, we can't save the people we love."

Max swallowed hard, the weight of Eli's words pressing into his chest. The truth of it was suffocating, but he couldn't bring himself to admit it. Not yet.

The silence that followed wasn't comforting. It was the kind that settled deep into the bones, a silence that came with too many things left unsaid. Max could feel the pull of it, the way it tried to drag him down into the depths of his own guilt.

They drove on, the silence between them stretching long and deep, until Max finally spoke, his voice barely above a whisper. "I made promises to her. Promises I couldn't keep."

Eli nodded, his eyes softening. "We all make promises like that. It's part of being human."

Max shook his head, bitterness creeping into his voice. "But I should have done more."

"You did everything you could," Eli said gently. "Sometimes, that has to be enough."

The words hung in the air, heavy with meaning, and for the first time in a long time, Max felt a crack in the armor he had built around himself. A part of him wanted to believe Eli, to accept that maybe, just maybe, he wasn't responsible for everything that had gone wrong.

But the guilt was too strong, too deeply embedded. And as much as he wanted to believe he wasn't to blame, another part of him knew that he would never be able to let it go.

The truck continued down the lonely road, swallowed by the night, the headlights cutting through the darkness like a thin, fragile lifeline. Max could feel the weight of the silence pressing in again, thicker now, more suffocating. There was no escaping it.

Chapter 7: The Shadows of His Father

Max kept his eyes on the road, the hum of the engine drowning out the noise in his mind. Eli sat quietly beside him, as usual, not saying much but always seeming to know more than Max was comfortable with. There had been moments in the silence where Max felt like Eli was waiting for him to speak, to open up, but Max wasn't sure where to begin.

But then, like the desert air itself, the memory crept in, uninvited but relentless.

Max could still remember the sharp crack of his father's voice cutting through the air like a whip.

"You fix your messes, Max," his father had said, standing in the garage, grease-stained hands gripping a wrench with the same intensity that Max had always felt wrapped around him. "No one's gonna clean up after you."

He had been just a boy back then, no more than ten years old, sitting on the edge of a workbench. His legs had dangled in the air, too short to reach the ground, while he watched his father move like a force of nature around the old Chevy truck that was always breaking down. The smell of gasoline and oil was thick in the air, mingling with the stale summer heat trapped inside the garage. Max hated the garage. It always felt like a place where mistakes were exposed, magnified under the scrutiny of his father's watchful eyes. There was no hiding in the garage—no space for error.

Max didn't fully understand engines, nor did he enjoy working on them as much as he did in the wood shop, where the scent of fresh-cut wood and the satisfying weight of a finished piece had always made him feel accomplished. But that didn't stop his father from making him learn. The tools were heavy in his small hands, and the instructions his father barked at him felt like another language entirely. Still, he scrambled to follow them, terrified of disappointing the man whose approval felt as distant as the stars.

He could still hear the sound of metal clanking against metal, the rhythmic scrape of his father's tools as he worked. The air had been thick, not just with the heat, but with unspoken expectations. Expectations that Max would one day grow into a man like his father—capable, unwavering, and utterly alone in his ability to solve problems.

His father had been a hard man, not one to sugarcoat the harsh realities of life. Max could still remember the way his father's calloused hands moved with certainty, every turn of the wrench deliberate and precise, as if fixing that old Chevy was a matter of life or death. His father never wavered, never showed hesitation, and that was what he expected from Max too.

"Why don't we just take it to the shop?" Max had asked, his voice small in the big, echoing space of the garage.

His father had slid out from beneath the truck, wiping his hands on an already dirty rag, and leveled his gaze at Max. Those eyes—dark and intense—held no room for weakness, no tolerance for shortcuts. "Because we don't let other people fix our problems," he had said. The words had felt like a commandment, a rule Max would carry with him long after that moment had passed.

Max had nodded, not fully understanding the weight of his father's words at the time, but even at ten, he had felt the gravity of the lesson pressing down on him. His father's lessons were always like that—heavy and impossible to ignore. They shaped him, molded him into the man he would become, for better or worse.

In the years that followed, that message had been drilled into him over and over again. His father was the type of man who believed in doing things yourself, never asking for help, and always taking responsibility for every little thing. It didn't matter if the problem was too big, or if the weight was too much to carry—if something went wrong, you fixed it. If someone needed saving, you saved them. There was no room for failure, no space for weakness, and certainly no time to wallow in self-pity.

The garage was a place of work and discipline. Max remembered the oppressive heat that seemed to close in on him every summer afternoon, the sun baking the metal roof until it felt like a furnace inside. His father would strip down to a tank top, his skin slick with sweat, and work tirelessly, muttering under his breath about faulty parts and useless mechanics. The air had always felt heavy in there, thick with the smell of gasoline and oil, as if the very atmosphere was saturated with frustration.

And there Max would be, a boy with hands too small for the wrench he was holding, doing his best to keep up. He had always tried to hide how much he struggled, but his father's sharp gaze had missed nothing. "Don't let that slip," his father would say, his voice hard but not cruel. It wasn't cruelty that defined his father—it was expectation. And those expectations had weighed on Max's shoulders like a yoke he could never quite shake off.

As the years passed, Max had grown to understand that his father wasn't just teaching him how to fix engines or patch up roofs—he was teaching him how to survive in a world that didn't care about excuses or second chances. His father was a man of few words, but the silence between them had always been filled with unspoken lessons. There were no long talks about feelings, no soft words of comfort when things got hard. There was only the expectation that Max would become the kind of man who could handle anything that came his way.

Max's jaw clenched as he thought about it now, the way his father's words had embedded themselves in his mind like iron nails. Fix your messes. Solve the problem. Don't ask for help. It was the way his father had lived, and it was the way Max had tried to live, even when it became impossible to bear.

Beside him, Eli remained silent, but Max could feel the weight of the man's presence pressing in on him, as if Eli knew exactly what Max was thinking about—exactly who he was thinking about.

"You don't have to carry it all by yourself," Eli said quietly, his voice cutting through the haze of memories that had wrapped around Max like a suffocating fog.

"What do you know about it?" he muttered, the words more defensive than he intended.

Eli's gaze shifted toward him, those dark, knowing eyes seeing far more than Max was comfortable with. "I know what it's like to carry the weight of someone else's expectations," Eli said, his voice calm but firm. "I know what it's like to feel like no matter what you do, it'll never be enough."

Max's heart pounded in his chest, the memories of his father, the old Chevy, and the garage swirling together with the present. The weight of his father's shadow had always been there, just out of sight, reminding him that he had to fix things, that he had to make things right, no matter the cost.

"I'm not running from my past," Max said, though even as the words left his mouth, they felt hollow.

Eli didn't argue. He just sat there, silent, letting the words hang in the air between them.

But Max knew better. He had been running from the shadows of his father, from the weight of the expectations that had been placed on him since he was a boy. He had been running from the guilt that came with every failure, every moment where he couldn't live up to the man his father had expected him to be.

And now, with Eli sitting beside him, Max couldn't help but wonder if he would ever stop running.

Chapter 8: The Shadows Between Us

The rain had slowed to a whisper now, tapping lightly on the roof of the truck as they moved deeper into the night. The weight of Eli's words lingered in the air, heavy and inescapable. Max kept his eyes on the road, but his thoughts were elsewhere—spiraling through the corridors of his past, where every turn seemed to lead back to Eve.

Eve. She had been everything to him, the one constant in a life that always felt like it was slipping through his fingers. Even as children, he had known there was something special about her. She had a light, a warmth that pulled him in, made him feel like maybe he wasn't destined to be just another person lost in the shuffle of the world. Even now, after all the time and distance that had separated them, he could still remember the way she used to laugh, the sound soft and musical, filling the air with something almost magical. Back then, it felt like Eve could turn even the bleakest days into something beautiful.

He remembered their long walks through the fields, her hand slipping into his, warm and small. The way her smile could chase away any darkness, and the way she believed in him, even when he didn't believe in himself. In her presence, Max felt seen—truly seen—and that had always been enough. Or at least, it had been.

But now that light was gone, and all that was left was darkness. Her absence was a void he couldn't seem to fill, a shadow that stretched across his life, no matter how hard he tried to move on. The memory of her lingered, like the scent of rain after a storm, faint but always there, always pulling him back to a time when things were simpler— when she was still there.

The truck's engine hummed softly, the only sound breaking the silence that had fallen between them. The headlights carved a narrow path through the night, illuminating the rain-slicked road, but Max's gaze flickered between the road ahead and the past behind him. Every thought seemed to circle back to that hospital room, to the sterile smell of antiseptic and the steady beeping of machines. Eve had been pale, her body fragile, but her smile had still been the same. Warm. Comforting. And, somehow, even in her weakest moments, she had found the strength to tell Max that it was okay—that everything would be okay.

But it hadn't been.

Max held ever so tight to the steering wheel as a flicker of guilt flared in his chest. He had done everything he could, hadn't he? Worked harder, taken out loans, begged doctors for miracles. And when all of that failed, when the money ran out and the treatments stopped working, he had crossed lines he'd promised himself he'd never cross. That was the part that haunted him the most—the way desperation had twisted his sense of right and wrong, how he had justified everything for the sake of saving her. The bank, the robbery, the gun. All for nothing.

The rain fell in a steady rhythm, but it felt distant, muted against the overwhelming silence between them. The night outside stretched on endlessly, the road disappearing into the horizon, swallowed by the shadows. There was something about the stillness in the truck that made Max's chest feel tight, like the air was too thick, too heavy. Every breath was labored, as though the weight of his past was slowly suffocating him.

He glanced at Eli, still sitting calmly beside him. The man's presence was both unsettling and comforting, as if he was supposed to be there but shouldn't exist at all. Eli seemed to know things without ever saying too much—knew how to dig beneath the surface, to peel away the layers Max had buried so deeply. There was something about Eli's stillness that made Max feel exposed, like every thought, every regret was laid bare for the man to see. It was as though Eli had been waiting for this moment—waiting for Max to finally break the silence.

"You ever wonder if there's a reason for all this?" Max asked, his voice barely above a whisper. He wasn't sure who he was asking—Eli or himself. "Like… maybe we're supposed to end up where we do, no matter what choices we make?"

The words hung in the air between them, heavy with the weight of unspoken truth. Max could hear his own heart beating in his chest, the steady thrum of the engine almost hypnotic as the truck rolled on through the night. The sound of the tires against the wet pavement created a steady rhythm, one that should have been calming, but instead only heightened the tension between them.

Eli didn't answer right away. He just stared out the window, his expression unreadable. The rain had slowed to a gentle drizzle, softening the world outside into blurred shapes and shadows. Max could hear the faint sound of water trickling through the gutters by the side of the road, the occasional rustle of wind through the trees. The world felt distant, muted, as if they were driving through some forgotten landscape that had been untouched by time.

"I think sometimes we end up where we're supposed to be, even if it doesn't feel like it. Even if we fight it."

Max frowned. "You really believe that?"

Eli's eyes slid back to Max, and for a brief moment, there was a flicker of something deeper in them—something ancient. Max could feel it in the way Eli held himself, the way his gaze seemed to pierce through the darkness and right into Max's soul. It was unsettling, the way Eli spoke with such certainty, as if he knew things that Max could only guess at. "I do."

Max swallowed hard, not sure how to respond. He wanted to believe it, wanted to believe that maybe, just maybe, all the mistakes he'd made had led him to something... meaningful. But it felt too much like wishful thinking. He'd seen too much, done too much, to put his faith in something so simple. His hands trembled on the wheel, the weight of his decisions pressing down on him, making his chest feel tight.

The road ahead seemed endless, stretching into the distance like a narrow bridge suspended over a void. The trees lining the road were dark silhouettes, their branches twisted and gnarled, reaching up into the sky as if trying to pull down the night itself. Max drove in silence, the tires splashing through puddles left behind by the storm. The shadows between the trees seemed to shift and move, playing tricks on his eyes. Every time he blinked, the world seemed to shift, and for a moment, he wasn't sure what was real anymore.

His thoughts circled back to the moment he'd pulled the trigger in that bank, the way the gun had felt so solid, so real in his hands. The way the sound had echoed, deafening, in the narrow hallway. He could still see the look in the eyes of the man he'd shot, the way the life had drained from him so quickly, so unexpectedly. That was the moment everything had changed. The moment he knew there was no going back. And now, sitting here with Eli, he wondered if that was the moment his fate had been sealed.

They drove in silence for a while longer, the road winding through hills and valleys, the night growing thicker around them. The shadows outside seemed to stretch farther, darker, as if the landscape itself was folding inward, closing them off from the rest of the world. Every bend in the road felt like a turn deeper into something unknown, a place where time and reality began to blur.

The headlights barely cut through the blackness, and Max felt a strange pull in his chest, a tightening that made it harder to breathe. He glanced in the rearview mirror, and for a split second, he thought he saw something—a figure, standing in the middle of the road, far behind them. But when he blinked, it was gone, swallowed by the night.

"You're feeling it, aren't you?" Eli's voice was soft, but there was something sharp beneath it.

Max's heart raced. "Feeling what?"

"The pull. The weight of it all." Eli turned to face him fully, his gaze piercing. "It's catching up to you, Max. You can't run from it forever."

Max's jaw clenched. "You keep saying that. What do you think I'm running from?"

Eli smiled, but it wasn't a comforting smile. It was the kind of smile you'd give someone when you knew something they didn't. "You know."

Chapter 9: The Price of Desperation

Max's hands tightened on the wheel, the hum of the engine blending with the rhythmic beat of his heart. His mind felt heavy, cluttered with the memories Eli had been dragging him back to. Each one came with more weight than the last, a burden he wasn't sure he could carry much longer.

It wasn't just the weight of what he had done, but the suffocating feeling that everything had been for nothing. Eve was gone. His desperation had led him down a path he never imagined he would walk, and in the end, it hadn't been enough. The decisions he had made in the name of love felt hollow now, each one a brick in the wall that had built up around his heart, separating him from the world.

Beside him, Eli sat quietly, his presence both soothing and unsettling. Max didn't want to look at him. He didn't want to see the knowing expression, the calm certainty in his eyes. Eli always seemed to know more than he let on, pulling at threads of memory that Max had long since buried. His silence was unnerving, as if Eli knew the exact moment to speak to bring Max's thoughts to the surface.

"I know what you're trying to do," Max said, his voice rough. "But it's not going to work."

He had spent years burying those memories, locking them away behind walls of anger and guilt. He didn't need Eli to dig them up now, to force him to confront the truth he had avoided for so long. Max clenched his teeth, his knuckles whitening as he gripped the wheel harder. But even as he spoke, he knew the words were hollow. Eli had already started the process, and Max could feel the cracks in his defenses widening with every passing moment.

Eli didn't answer right away. The silence stretched out between them, thick and uncomfortable. Max could feel Eli watching him, waiting for the right moment to strike. The tension in the air was palpable, pressing down on him like a weight he couldn't shake off. He didn't want to admit it, but Eli had a way of making him face things he didn't want to face—things he had spent years trying to forget.

"It wasn't just about love, was it?" Eli's voice was soft, cutting through the quiet like a knife. "You thought it would be enough. But when did you realize it wasn't?"

Max clenched his jaw tighter, his hands pulsing as he gripped the steering wheel. He didn't want to answer, didn't want to go back to that moment, but Eli had a way of prying the truth out of him. The memories were painful, sharp-edged, cutting into him even after all this time. The desperation, the fear—it had all come rushing back the moment Eli brought it up.

Max swallowed hard, the lump in his throat nearly choking him.

"It was the day we got the final diagnosis," Max whispered. "The day the doctor said the word 'terminal.' That's when I knew… love wasn't enough."

***

The doctor's words echoed in his mind: Terminal. Nothing more we can do.

Max had sat there, numb, unable to process what the doctor had just said. His world had collapsed in an instant, the future he had imagined with Eve shattering like glass. The sterile smell of the hospital room seemed to suffocate him, the steady beeping of machines a cruel reminder of the life slipping away from him.

The world had gone blurry around him, the only thing he could focus on was the thought that there had to be something more. There had to be another option. His mind had raced, frantically searching for a way out, a way to keep her with him. But every road led back to the same harsh reality: Eve was dying, and there was nothing he could do to stop it.

But there wasn't. The treatments had failed. The money was gone. And Eve… Eve was slipping away from him. Max had spent countless nights lying awake beside her, listening to the soft rasp of her breathing, wondering how much time they had left. Each day felt like a countdown to the inevitable, and no matter how hard he tried, he couldn't stop the clock from ticking.

That night, as he sat beside her in the darkened hospital room, Max made a decision. He would do whatever it took. He wasn't ready to lose her, and if money was what they needed, he would find it. No matter what it cost. The thought had gripped him with an intensity that scared him, a desperation that consumed him. Love hadn't been enough, but maybe, just maybe, money could buy them more time.

Eli's voice pulled him back to the present.

"You thought you could fix it, didn't you?" Eli asked quietly. "You thought if you just found the right solution, you could save her."

Max blinked, his throat tightening. "I didn't have a choice."

"There's always a choice," Eli replied softly. "But you didn't want to admit that the one thing you couldn't fix was her."

Max's heart pounded in his chest as he turned to Eli, the weight of those words settling over him like a suffocating blanket. He could still feel the desperation that had gripped him that night—the burning need to do something, anything, to keep her alive. The memory of sitting in that hospital room, staring at Eve's pale face, haunted him. He had promised her that he would find a way, that he wouldn't give up. But in the end, all his promises had been empty.

"It wasn't for me," Max muttered, almost defensively. "It was for her."

Eli's gaze never wavered. "Was it?"

***

Max paced in the small apartment, the worn carpet soft under his feet. Eve was asleep in the bedroom, her breathing shallow but steady. The moonlight filtered through the blinds, casting long shadows across the room. The night was quiet, too quiet, the kind of stillness that made every sound seem louder, more significant. The ticking of the clock on the wall was like a countdown, each second slipping away, taking Eve with it.

On the coffee table in front of him lay the hospital bills. Stacks of them. Unpaid. Overdue. He had tried everything —double shifts, selling off their belongings, maxing out their credit cards—but nothing was enough. The medical costs were insurmountable, and the insurance had long since run out. Max felt the weight of it crushing him, pressing down on him from all sides. The walls of the apartment felt too close, too confining, like they were closing in on him.

His eyes drifted to the kitchen counter, where a crumpled flyer lay, advertising loans with "no questions asked." Max had already called every number he could think of, but they all wanted something he didn't have. He had run out of options.

That's when he saw it.

A small news story playing on the TV, barely a headline: Local Bank Sees Security Cutbacks Due to Budget Issues.

The idea was small at first, just a whisper in the back of his mind. But it grew. He sat down, staring at the bills, the weight of them crushing him. He could rob the bank. It wasn't a big bank—just a small-town branch with a skeleton crew. He could be in and out before anyone even knew what happened. The thought scared him, but it also gave him a strange sense of hope. Maybe this was the answer. Maybe this was the way to save her.

It would be enough to pay for more treatments. Enough to keep Eve alive.

Max snapped out of the memory, his breath catching in his throat. His chest felt tight, as if the walls of the truck were closing in on him.

Chapter 10: The Mask of Normalcy

The desert lengthened endlessly ahead, the sky a burnt orange as the sun dipped below the horizon. Max kept his eyes on the road, but his mind was elsewhere—trapped between the world he was running from and the lies he had built to survive it. The landscape outside the truck was vast, but Max felt cornered, his thoughts closing in on him like walls.

The weight of everything he'd done—the secrets, the fear, the decisions he couldn't undo—pressed on him, making the vast openness of the desert feel like a prison.

Beside him, Eli sat in his usual quiet, a presence that gnawed at Max's thoughts like a persistent itch he couldn't reach. Max could feel Eli's eyes on him, watching, waiting. There were no words between them, but the weight of unspoken truths pressed down harder with each passing mile. Eli had a way of making silence feel oppressive, as though each second that passed was another thread tightening around Max's neck, pulling him closer to the edge.

"Was it hard?" Eli's voice broke the silence, calm and composed as ever. "Living two lives?"

Max flinched, He didn't answer at first, unsure of how to respond. He didn't like the way Eli asked these questions, as if he already knew the answers but wanted Max to admit them aloud. The truth was, it had been hard—much harder than Max ever thought it would be. But saying that out loud felt like admitting failure.

Eli waited, his gaze steady, as if he already knew the answer.

"It wasn't supposed to be two lives," Max muttered, his voice low. "At first, I thought I could handle it. Keep everything separate."

Eli raised an eyebrow, his silence urging Max to continue.

Max swallowed, the memories creeping back like shadows in the fading light. The delicate balancing act he had tried to maintain between his life with Eve and the dark, desperate plan he was concocting. It had been fragile from the start, but he had convinced himself that he could keep everything under control, that he could protect Eve from the truth.

"How long did that last?" Eli's voice was soft, but the question felt like a blow.

Max's jaw clenched as he thought about how quickly it had all started to unravel. The moment he decided to take that path, to plan the robbery, something had shifted. The life he had with Eve, the life that had once felt so simple and good, began to slip through his fingers.

****

Max stood at the stove, stirring a pot of soup. The smell of chicken broth filled the air, mixing with the sound of soft music playing from the radio. It was one of Eve's favorite songs—an old tune they used to dance to in their living room when life still felt like it had possibilities. The melody had always brought a smile to her face, but now, even the music felt hollow, a reminder of better days they couldn't get back.

He glanced over at the couch, where Eve lay under a blanket, her body thin and frail. She had fallen asleep, her breathing shallow but peaceful. For a moment, Max allowed himself to believe that everything was normal. That they were just an ordinary couple spending a quiet evening at home. He tried to pretend that nothing had changed, that they weren't drowning under the weight of bills and the cruel reality of her illness.

But the stack of bills on the counter told a different story. Each one a reminder of the impossible debt they had accumulated. The unpaid medical bills that loomed over them like a storm cloud. Max had done everything he could to stay on top of it, to keep the worry from showing in his face when Eve asked if they were okay.

He stirred the soup absentmindedly, his mind already drifting to the plan he'd been perfecting. He had memorized the layout of the bank, studied the staff, timed the shifts. Every detail had to be precise. He couldn't afford any mistakes. Not with so much at stake. He thought about the way he would walk into that bank, the mask he would wear, the way his voice would sound when he demanded the money. Every scenario had played out in his mind a hundred times.

The knock on the door startled him, pulling him from his thoughts. He quickly turned the burner down and wiped his hands on a dish towel, his heart thudding in his chest. As he opened the door, he forced a smile onto his face.

It was the neighbor, Mrs. Kelley, holding a basket of freshly baked cookies. "I just wanted to drop these off for you and Eve," she said, her smile warm but her eyes filled with concern. Max could see the pity in her eyes, the way she looked at him as if he was a man carrying the world on his shoulders.

"How's she doing?"

Max nodded, his practiced response slipping from his lips. "She's hanging in there. We're doing everything we can."

Mrs. Kelley's eyes softened. "You're such a strong husband, Max. It must be so hard."

Max forced another smile, the words twisting inside him like a knife. If only she knew. If only anyone knew what he was really doing. "We'll get through it," he said, his voice tight. "One way or another."

As soon as the door closed behind her, Max's smile vanished. He leaned against the doorframe, closing his eyes for a moment. The mask he had been wearing slipped just a little, the weight of his double life pressing down on him. How long could he keep this up? How long before everything came crashing down around him?

Eli's voice pulled him back to the present.

"You thought you could keep it all together, didn't you?" Eli asked, his tone almost sympathetic. "Hide the cracks, make everyone think everything was fine."

Max stared straight ahead, his jaw clenched. "I didn't have a choice. No one could know."

"And what about Eve?" Eli's voice softened. "Did she know?"

Max's breath hitched, his heart squeezing in his chest. He had tried so hard to keep everything from her. But there were moments—small, fleeting moments—when he wondered if she had started to see through the cracks in his armor.

***

Max sat at the kitchen table late one night, the soft hum of the refrigerator the only sound in the room. A small notebook lay open in front of him, filled with scribbled notes and diagrams of the bank. He flipped through the pages, his brow furrowed in concentration. The plan had to be perfect. No room for error. The stakes were too high.

Every step of the robbery had to be calculated, from the moment he walked into the bank to the exact minute he would leave. He couldn't afford any mistakes, not when Eve's life was hanging in the balance. The money would save her. It had to.

He didn't hear Eve until she spoke.

"Max?" Her voice was soft, barely above a whisper.

Max jolted, quickly shutting the notebook and sliding it under a pile of papers. He looked up, forcing a smile. "Hey, you're awake. How are you feeling?"

Eve stood in the doorway, her eyes tired but alert. She watched him for a long moment, her brow furrowing slightly. "What were you working on?"

"Just… bills," Max lied, his heart racing. He stood up, crossing the room to guide her back toward the couch. "You shouldn't be up. You need to rest."

Eve let him lead her, but she didn't look convinced. She glanced back at the table, her gaze lingering on the pile of papers he had hastily covered. Max's stomach twisted with guilt. She was too tired to push further, but he could see the question in her eyes—the one she hadn't asked yet. He saw the flicker of doubt in her expression, the way her eyes seemed to search his for answers she wasn't sure she wanted.

She leaned into him, her voice barely a whisper. "You're not… hiding anything from me, are you?"

The words hit him like a punch to the gut. He hesitated for a split second, long enough for doubt to creep in, before forcing the lie. "Of course not, Eve. You know I'd never keep anything from you."

Eve nodded, but the look in her eyes told him she wasn't entirely convinced. She settled back into the couch, closing her eyes as Max wrapped the blanket around her. He kissed her forehead, his heart heavy with the weight of his secret.

In the truck, Max's breath came out in short, shallow bursts. He hadn't wanted to remember that night—the look in Eve's eyes, the doubt she tried to push away. She had trusted him, even when she knew something wasn't right.

"I tried to protect her," Max whispered, more to himself than to Eli. "I didn't want her to worry. I didn't want her to know."

Eli's gaze was steady. "But she did know. Didn't she?"

Max swallowed hard, the guilt clawing at him. He had seen it in her eyes—Eve's quiet suspicion, the way she watched him when she thought he wasn't looking. She hadn't wanted to ask because she hadn't wanted to know the truth. She had trusted him because she had to, but deep down, she had known something was wrong.

***

Max stood in the shadows of the bank, his eyes scanning the empty parking lot. He had driven by the bank every night for the past week, memorizing every detail. The security cameras. The exits. The way the light flickered near the back door.

He pulled the collar of his jacket up, shivering against the cold. His breath came out in short, sharp bursts as he watched the night shift employees leave. The skeleton crew. It would be easy. In and out. No one would even know until it was too late.

His phone buzzed in his pocket, startling him. Max pulled it out, seeing Eve's name flash across the screen. He hesitated, staring at the phone in his hand. She was probably wondering where he was. He had told her he was running errands, but deep down, he knew she didn't believe him.

His thumb hovered over the answer button for a moment before he slipped the phone back into his pocket. He couldn't talk to her now. Not when he was standing on the edge of something he couldn't come back from.

For now, it was just another step in the plan, another rehearsal for the moment he could no longer avoid.

"You thought you could live two lives," Eli said, his voice soft but firm. "But in the end, you can't hide the truth forever. Not from her. Not from yourself."

Max's heart pounded in his chest as Eli's words sank in. He could feel the truth closing in on him, suffocating him.

"I didn't have a choice," Max whispered, his voice shaking.

But even as the words left his lips, he wasn't sure he believed them anymore.

Chapter 11: Beneath the Surface

The truck's headlights cut through the darkness, the desert stretching out on either side of the road like a void. The night seemed endless, the road beneath them disappearing into the shadows as if there was no destination. Max's mind was heavy with memories, each one a weight pressing harder against his chest. The present felt distant, as if the truck was moving through time rather than space, pulling him back into moments he wished he could forget.

He didn't speak, didn't even glance at Eli, though he could feel Eli's eyes on him, as if waiting for the next secret to be pulled from the depths. Eli had a way of being silent that made Max's own thoughts seem deafening, the quiet between them louder than any words. Each mile felt heavier, as if the road was taking him deeper into the recesses of his mind, where the truth waited to be confronted.

"You planned every detail," Eli's voice finally broke the silence, calm and steady. His tone was almost casual, as if they were discussing the weather, not the events that had led Max to the edge. "Every step. Like you were trying to control the uncontrollable."

Max's grip on the wheel tightened, his fingers digging in deep. He knew where Eli was taking him, and he didn't want to go there. But the memories were already rising to the surface, the ones he had tried to bury for months. He had told himself the robbery was for Eve—that every desperate decision he made was to save her. But the truth was darker than that.

"It had to be perfect," Max whispered, his voice hollow. "No mistakes."

***

Max sat in the dimly lit backroom of a pawnshop, his hands trembling as he held the gun in his lap. The metal was cold against his skin, unfamiliar, and somehow that was comforting. He couldn't bring himself to use the guns he already owned. They had belonged to his father—kept locked away in the house for years. There was no way he could use them for this.

He had stared at those guns for days, trying to convince himself that it would be okay. But every time he touched the wooden handle of his father's rifle or the old revolver he had taught Max to shoot with as a boy, the guilt crept in. It was like using those guns would betray everything his father had tried to teach him about right and wrong.

So, he had come here, to this dingy little shop on the edge of town, where no one asked questions and everything had a price. The gun he held was sleek, black, efficient—nothing like the heavy, weathered revolvers he was used to. The weight of it felt foreign in his hands, but at the same time, it made everything real. This was no longer just a plan; it was something tangible, something dangerous.

"You sure about this one?" the shopkeeper asked, his voice gruff, his eyes sharp beneath bushy brows. "It's clean, no trace. But it's not a toy. You ready for that?"

Max nodded, his throat tight. "Yeah. I'm ready."

He wasn't, not really. But he couldn't afford to hesitate. Not now. Not with Eve's life slipping through his fingers. The desperation that had driven him to this place was like a fire in his veins, burning away any remnants of doubt. He had to be ready, because if he wasn't, Eve would die. And that was a reality he couldn't face.

The sound of the pawnshop's door closing behind him echoed in his ears long after he left. The gun, now tucked inside his jacket, felt heavier with each step he took. It wasn't just the weight of the metal; it was the weight of what it represented. The point of no return.

***

The engine of his truck hummed quietly as Max parked across the street from the bank, hidden behind a row of trees. He had been here every day for the past two weeks, watching, memorizing the routine. The bank was small, unassuming—a skeleton crew of employees, no real security to speak of. It should have been easy. It had to be.

He pulled a small notebook from the glove compartment, flipping it open to the worn pages filled with sketches, notes, and calculations. The layout of the bank was etched into his mind, every inch of the building accounted for. He knew when the security guard took his breaks, which exit doors were rarely used, and which streets he could disappear down when it was over.

Max's pen hovered over the page, making small adjustments to the escape route he had planned. He couldn't afford to be sloppy. Every second counted. He had mapped out the backstreets, memorized the traffic patterns at different times of day, and scouted several places where he could ditch the truck if he needed to. Every detail had to be perfect. He told himself this over and over, clinging to the illusion of control like a lifeline.

His eyes flicked up to the bank's entrance. A woman walked out, chatting with one of the tellers as she locked the door behind her. The bank closed early on Fridays—a detail he'd picked up after the first week. Another advantage.

In and out. That's what he kept telling himself. In and out, and no one gets hurt.

But the knot in his stomach told him it wouldn't be that simple.

Max leaned back in his seat, the tension in his body refusing to release. He watched the woman laugh, her carefree expression a stark contrast to the storm brewing inside him. She didn't know what was coming. No one did. And that was the hardest part—knowing that his actions, no matter how well-intentioned, would leave a trail of consequences he couldn't predict.

The memory of those drives lingered in Max's mind, his chest tightening with the weight of it. Eli hadn't said a word, but Max could feel him watching, waiting. He didn't need to say anything. The memories spoke for themselves.

"You spent weeks planning," Eli said quietly. "Driving past that bank over and over. You thought if you could control every detail, you could make it right. But it wasn't about the plan, was it?"

Max breathing deeply, his fingers white on the steering wheel. "I didn't want it to go wrong. I couldn't afford it to go wrong."

***

The sporting goods store was empty, save for the clerk behind the counter, who barely glanced at Max as he walked in. Max's eyes scanned the shelves, his heart pounding in his chest. He wasn't here for a gun, not this time. He was here for something simpler. Something to hide his face.

The mask section was tucked in the corner of the store, next to the hunting gear. He stared at the rows of ski masks, the shelves filled with balaclavas and face coverings. His hands shook as he reached for one—a plain black mask that would hide everything but his eyes.

It was a simple thing, just a piece of fabric. But holding it made everything feel real in a way it hadn't before. This wasn't just a plan anymore. This was happening. The realization hit him like a punch to the gut. He wasn't just preparing for something abstract—he was about to cross a line he could never uncross.

Max grabbed the mask and headed for the counter, his footsteps heavy. The cashier barely looked up as he scanned the item and shoved it into a bag. Max's heart raced as he handed over the cash, his hands slick with sweat. The mask, now hidden in the plastic bag, felt like a weight he couldn't shake. It was a symbol of everything he was about to do, everything he was willing to sacrifice.

Max exhaled sharply in the truck, his mind spinning. He could still feel the weight of that mask in his hands, the way it had felt so small and insignificant—until it wasn't. He hadn't told anyone about the mask. He hadn't even told himself why he chose it. But Eli knew. Somehow, Eli always knew.

"You planned every detail," Eli said softly, his voice cutting through the silence. "But when the time came, you left the mask at home."

Max flinched, the words hitting him like a punch to the gut. He hadn't meant to forget it. He had been so careful, so precise about everything. The mask had been the last piece of the plan, the thing that would keep him anonymous. And yet, on the day of the robbery, it had stayed in his kitchen drawer, forgotten in the rush.

"It was almost like you wanted people to know it was you," Eli continued, his voice quiet but unrelenting. "Like you wanted credit for what you were about to do."

Max shook his head, his chest tight with guilt. "No. I didn't want anyone to know. It wasn't about that."

"Wasn't it?" Eli's gaze was steady, piercing. "You left the mask behind. Maybe deep down, you wanted someone to see you. To understand that this wasn't just a crime. It was something more. Something you were willing to do because of how much you loved her."

Max swallowed hard, his throat dry. He had spent so long telling himself that the robbery was for Eve—that every choice, every step was for her. But now, with Eli's words hanging in the air, he wasn't so sure. Had he left the mask behind on purpose? Had part of him wanted to be seen, to be recognized for the lengths he had gone to for her?

***

Max pulled the truck up to the bank, his hands trembling as he turned off the engine. The bank was only a few miles away, the plan already set in motion. But as he sat there in the driver's seat, staring at the door to the bank It hit him, he wasn't wearing the mask.

His fingers twitched toward the glove compartment, where it should have been. But he hadn't brought it with him. In the rush to leave, he had forgotten. And now, as he sat there, ready to rob a bank, ready to do the one thing he swore he'd never do… it didn't seem to matter anymore.

It's for her, he told himself again, his heart pounding in his chest. It's all for her.

But as the minutes ticked by, and the weight of what he was about to do pressed down on him, Max couldn't shake the feeling that maybe—just maybe—it was also for him.

"You didn't forget the mask, Max," Eli said softly. "You left it behind. Because deep down, you wanted someone to see you. To know that you were willing to do anything. Even this."

Max's chest tightened, the truth settling over him like a heavy weight. He could still feel the gun in his hands, the cold metal biting into his skin. He had told himself it was for Eve. But now, in the quiet of the night, with Eli's eyes watching him, he wasn't sure what he believed anymore.

"I didn't have a choice," Max whispered, his voice shaking.

But the words felt hollow. Because deep down, he knew that he had made a choice long before the robbery ever took place.

Chapter 12: The Truth in the Dark

Max sat in the stillness, the truck parked on the side of the road as the world outside seemed to press in on him. The darkness felt heavier now, more oppressive, like it was trying to suffocate him. His heart pounded in his chest, the echo of Eli's words reverberating in his mind.

You stop running. You face it. And you let go.

But what did that even mean? How could he stop running when the truth he was running from felt like a blade pressed to his throat? The memories, the pain, the loss—they had defined him for so long. Without them, who was he?

The air inside the truck was thick, oppressive. The faint smell of rain lingered, mixing with the old leather seats and the scent of dust from the road. It felt like the entire world was pressing down on him, suffocating him in his silence. Max's hands gripped the steering wheel tightly, as if holding on to the wheel would somehow anchor him, keep him from unraveling completely.

Eli hadn't moved, his eyes steady on Max, as if waiting for him to make a decision. His presence was unsettling, but not in a way that made Max want to push him away. It was more like Eli was something inevitable—like he had always been there, waiting for Max to notice.

The truck's interior felt suffocating, as if the weight of his past, the guilt he had carried for so long, was too much for the small space. The air seemed thick, heavy with tension and things left unsaid. Outside, the road was silent, the rain now just a memory, leaving only the dark, slick pavement stretching endlessly in front of them. The quiet between them wasn't just silence—it was a void, pregnant with expectation.

Max exhaled, his breath shaky. "I don't know if I can do this," he admitted, his voice barely above a whisper.

Eli didn't respond immediately. Instead, he leaned forward slightly, his eyes narrowing in that intense, unsettling way he had. His gaze felt like it pierced through every wall Max had built, every barrier he had used to protect himself. "What are you afraid of?"

The question hung in the air, and for a moment, Max considered not answering. But he could feel Eli's gaze on him, feel the weight of the truth pressing down on his chest. It was like the man had already seen through him— knew the answer before Max could even admit it to himself.

Max clenched his jaw, the words bubbling up inside him before he could stop them. "Losing her. Losing everything. Losing… myself."

His voice cracked on the last word, and Max winced. He hadn't meant to say that. But once the words were out, he couldn't pull them back. They hung between them, heavy and raw, the truth he had been running from for so long.

Eli's gaze didn't waver. "But you already did."

The statement hit Max like a punch to the gut, stealing the air from his lungs. He wanted to argue, to fight against the truth Eli had laid bare, but the man was right. He had already lost everything. Eve was gone. The life they had built was gone. And the person he used to be? That version of Max had died with her, in the sterile white walls of the hospital room, with the endless beeping of machines that could no longer save her.

Max's throat tightened, and he felt the sting of tears he didn't want to shed. He had spent so long burying that pain, running from it, drowning it in his desperation to fix things. But there was no fixing this. No going back.

The weight of his loss pressed down on him like a physical force, crushing him beneath the memories, the what-ifs, and the regrets. His chest felt tight, the air in the truck too thin, too stale. He hadn't been ready to face this—not now, not here. But it seemed like the universe, through Eli, had forced him to confront what he had been running from for so long.

Eli leaned back, his voice softer now. "The longer you run, the farther you get from yourself."

Max blinked, fighting back the emotion that threatened to break through. "What do you want me to do?" His voice cracked, betraying him. He didn't know what he was asking anymore—whether he was pleading with Eli for guidance, or if he was begging himself to finally let go.

Eli turned his gaze toward the road ahead, his expression unreadable. The road stretched into darkness, illuminated only by the faint glow of the truck's headlights. "You're asking the wrong question."

Max frowned. "What's the right question?"

"The right question is what you want to do," Eli said, his voice quiet but firm. "What do you want, Max?"

The simplicity of the question hit Max harder than he expected. What did he want? He hadn't thought about that in so long. It had always been about what needed to be done—what he had to do for Eve, for their future, for survival. Want had disappeared from his vocabulary the day Eve's diagnosis had turned their world upside down.

Max shook his head, frustration bubbling to the surface. "What I want doesn't matter. It never did. It's too late."

Eli's eyes flicked back to him, sharp and unwavering. "It's only too late if you keep telling yourself it is."

The silence between them stretched, heavy and thick with unspoken truths. Max felt like he was teetering on the edge of something—something he couldn't quite name but knew was important. He had been carrying this weight for so long, dragging it with him through every bad decision, every mistake, every moment of desperation.

But what if Eli was right? What if the only thing holding him back was himself?

His mind flashed back to those days with Eve. She had always been the one to center him, to pull him out of the fog of self-doubt that seemed to constantly cloud his vision. But the memory of her felt farther away now, like trying to reach through smoke. The hospital visits, the long nights of waiting for news that never got better—it all felt so distant, yet it was still the anchor that kept him from moving forward.

Max's mind flashed again to the past—to that classroom where he and Eve had first connected, where their friendship had blossomed into something more. He remembered the way she had laughed at his jokes, the way she had always been able to pull him out of his own head when he got too caught up in the world's harshness.

But now, even in his memories, Eve felt distant, unreachable. Like she had already slipped beyond his grasp, and he was just chasing the ghost of her.

Max tightened his grip once more on the wheel as he stared out into the darkness. "It's all just… gone," he muttered, more to himself than to Eli. "I couldn't save her."

Eli's voice was soft but firm, cutting through the quiet. "You couldn't save her. But maybe she didn't need you to."

Max's chest ached at those words. He had spent every waking moment trying to save her, trying to make things right. How could Eli say something like that?

"What are you talking about?" Max asked, his voice hoarse. "Of course she needed me. She was dying."

Eli turned his gaze back to Max, and there was something deep and unsettling in his eyes—something that made Max feel like he was standing on the precipice of something far bigger than he could understand. "She needed you to be with her, Max. Not to fix things. Just to be with her."

Max stared at him, the truth of those words sinking in. How many times had Eve told him that? How many times had she tried to get him to just sit with her, to hold her hand, to be there? But he had always been too focused on fixing things, on finding the solution, on making everything right.

And in the end, he had missed the most important part.

"I—" Max's voice faltered, the weight of his regret threatening to crush him. "I didn't know how."

Eli's expression softened, and for the first time, Max saw something close to sympathy in his eyes. "It's not too late to know now."

Max swallowed hard, his throat thick with emotion. He didn't know if he could do this. Didn't know if he could face everything he had buried. But as he sat there, the silence between them growing heavier, he realized something he hadn't allowed himself to admit.

He didn't want to keep running. Not anymore.

Max's hands loosened on the steering wheel as he let out a long, shaky breath. "I don't know where to start."

Eli smiled, just a hint of one, and it was enough. "You already have."

The road ahead stretched out, dark and uncertain, but for the first time in what felt like forever, Max didn't feel the need to run from it. Maybe Eli was right. Maybe it wasn't too late to face the truth.

Max started the engine again, the hum of the truck filling the space around them. He didn't know where the road was leading him, but it didn't matter anymore. He was ready to face whatever was waiting.

Chapter 13: What Lies Beneath

The road stretched endlessly ahead, an unforgiving line that seemed to lead nowhere and everywhere all at once. Max drove in silence, his thoughts a chaotic swirl of memories, regrets, and half-formed realizations. The hum of the engine was the only sound between them, but even that felt distant, like white noise on the edge of consciousness.

The sky above was a bruised shade of black, the horizon stretching out like a wound across the landscape, bleeding shadows over the hills. Every mile the truck ate up felt like a step deeper into an abyss. The air inside the truck was thick, heavy with unspoken words and the ghosts of memories Max didn't want to confront. He could feel the weight of those ghosts pressing down on him, and yet, no matter how far he drove, he couldn't seem to outrun them.

The stillness of the night was unnerving, a kind of silence that felt too loud. The wind had died down, leaving the world outside the truck eerily calm. It was as if the entire desert had paused, waiting for something to happen. Max's heart raced despite the quiet, each beat a reminder of the tension inside him, the unresolved emotions that had been festering for too long. His body felt tight, wound up with a nervous energy that had nowhere to go.

Beside him, Eli sat motionless, his face cast in shadow as the night pressed in around them. Max could feel his presence, steady and unwavering, like a quiet pressure in the back of his mind. Eli had a way of filling the silence without speaking, his mere presence forcing Max to confront everything he had been avoiding for so long. There was no escape with Eli there—no way to shove down the memories or pretend they didn't exist.

Eli wasn't like anyone Max had ever known. There was something about him that felt old, timeless even, like he had seen the rise and fall of civilizations. Max had picked up strangers before, but Eli didn't feel like a stranger at all. He felt familiar, like someone who had been there all along, waiting for the right moment to reveal himself.

Max's chest felt heavy, the weight of his past choices pressing down on him. How many times had he run from the truth? How many times had he tried to fix things, only to make them worse? The road ahead looked the same, but in Max's mind, he was traveling back through time, revisiting every moment that had led him to this point.

His mind drifted back to Eve, as it always did. The hospital room, the beeping machines, the sterile smell of antiseptic that still haunted him in his dreams. He could see her lying there, pale and fragile, her body so small against the white sheets. The memory was so vivid it hurt—her face gaunt, her eyes dull but still filled with that same love she always had for him.

The final days had been the hardest. He had sat beside her, watching her slip away, powerless to stop it. The doctors had stopped coming in with new treatment plans, and the nurses no longer spoke in hopeful tones. The atmosphere in the room had changed from one of urgency to resignation. Max had refused to accept it. Every day he had told himself there was still time, that something could be done. But Eve had known better. She had known, long before he did, that there was no saving her.

And Max—stubborn, determined, desperate—had refused to accept it. He had fought, harder than he had ever fought for anything, to save her. But some battles aren't meant to be won. Some battles are meant to teach you how to lose.

You don't have to fix this, Max. Just be here with me.

Her voice echoed in his mind, soft and distant, like a memory he couldn't quite grasp. He had tried to save her, tried to find a way to make everything right. But in the end, all she had ever wanted was for him to be there. And he hadn't been. Not in the way she needed.

The memory of Eve's voice made Max's chest tighten, a deep ache settling in his bones. He had failed her. He had failed to give her what she needed most in her final days. He had been so focused on finding a solution, on fixing the unfixable, that he hadn't been present with her. And now, with her gone, all he had left was the crushing weight of that failure.

The guilt gnawed at him, a familiar ache that had never quite gone away. It was a constant companion now, like a shadow that followed him no matter how far he tried to run.

He had taken everything into his hands, believing that if he could just control the situation, he could save her. But life had other plans. The weight of failure pressed against his chest like a stone, heavy and immovable. It was like trying to outrun the tide—no matter how far you go, it always catches up to you.

"You're thinking about her again, aren't you?"

Eli's voice cut through the silence, soft but sharp, as if he had pulled the thoughts directly from Max's mind. Max glanced at him, unsure of how to respond. There was no point in denying it. Of course he was thinking about her. He was always thinking about her.

The memories of Eve were a double-edged sword. They brought him comfort, but they also ripped him apart. Every image of her smile, every echo of her laughter, was a reminder of what he had lost—and what he had failed to save.

"Yeah," Max muttered, his voice low. "I'm always thinking about her."

Eli nodded, his gaze steady. There was something in the way Eli looked at him that made Max feel exposed, like Eli could see every part of him, even the parts he tried to keep hidden. "And what do you see when you think about her?"

Max frowned, his thoughts stumbling over the question. What did he see? He saw the good times, of course. The way she had laughed, the way her smile could light up a room. But more than that, he saw the hospital. The machines. The way her body had grown weaker with each passing day.

"I see what I lost," Max said finally, his voice thick with emotion. "I see what I couldn't save."

Eli didn't respond right away. He seemed to be weighing Max's words, turning them over in his mind. When he spoke again, his voice was soft, almost gentle. "Do you ever see what you still have?"

Max blinked, confused. "What are you talking about? I don't have anything left."

Eli's eyes met his, piercing through the darkness. "You still have her, Max. Not in the way you wanted, maybe. But she's still with you."

Max felt a lump rise in his throat. He wanted to argue, to push back against what Eli was saying. But deep down, he knew there was truth in those words. Eve was still with him —her memory, her love. It had never left him. Even when he tried to drown it in guilt and regret, she was still there, a quiet presence in the back of his mind.

Max shifted in his seat, the weight of those memories bearing down on him. He could still feel her—like she was sitting beside him in the truck, just out of reach. It was maddening, that closeness, that sense of her still lingering. He couldn't decide if it was a comfort or a curse.

"She wouldn't want you to keep running," Eli added, his voice steady. "She wouldn't want you to keep punishing yourself for something you couldn't control."

Max swallowed hard, the sting of tears threatening to break through. He had held onto that guilt for so long that he didn't know how to live without it. He didn't know who he was without it. "But I should've done more. I should've been there for her. I—"

"You were there," Eli interrupted, his voice firm but kind. "Maybe not in the way you thought you needed to be, but you were there. She knew you loved her, Max. That's all she ever needed."

Max's heart ached at those words, a pain so deep and raw that he could barely breathe. He had spent so long trying to fix things, to make up for the things he couldn't change. But maybe, just maybe, Eli was right. Maybe Eve hadn't needed him to be perfect. Maybe she had just needed him to love her.

The road ahead stretched out into the darkness, but for the first time in a long time, Max didn't feel the urge to run from it. He didn't feel the need to escape the weight of his past. Instead, he felt a strange sense of peace, like a quiet settling over his soul.

"I don't know how to let go," Max admitted, his voice barely above a whisper.

Eli leaned back in his seat, his eyes still on Max. "You don't have to let go. You just have to stop holding on so tightly."

Max stared ahead, his mind reeling. He had been holding on so tightly to his guilt, his regret, that he hadn't even realized how much it was suffocating him. Maybe Eli was right. Maybe it wasn't about letting go. Maybe it was about loosening his grip, about allowing himself to breathe again.

The truck rolled on, the hum of the engine filling the space between them. Max's thoughts drifted, circling around the truth he had been avoiding for so long. He didn't want to keep running. He didn't want to keep punishing himself for things he couldn't change.

"I just want to be free of it," Max said, his voice low and broken.

Eli turned to him, a soft smile playing on his lips. "Then maybe it's time to forgive yourself."

The words hit Max like a punch to the gut, stealing the air from his lungs. Forgive himself? Could he even do that?

After everything that had happened, after everything he had lost… could he really find it in himself to let go of the blame?

Max wasn't sure. But as the truck rumbled forward, carrying him deeper into the night, he knew one thing for certain.

He didn't want to keep running.

Not anymore.

Chapter 14: The Weight of Memory

The night stretched long and quiet, the hum of the truck's engine a steady, comforting noise that filled the silence between them. Max kept his hands on the steering wheel, his eyes fixed on the road ahead, but his mind was drifting somewhere far behind—back into a past that felt both distant and immediate.

The road ahead seemed endless, a dark ribbon winding through an empty landscape. The headlights of the truck barely pierced the gloom, and the darkness beyond was like a shroud, enveloping them in its quiet embrace. The world outside had shrunk to the narrow beam of light cast in front of them, but inside the truck, the weight of unspoken memories hung heavy in the air.

Eli hadn't said a word in what felt like hours. He didn't need to. Max could feel his presence beside him, steady and watchful, like a shadow that knew more than it should. It was as if Eli was waiting, patiently biding his time, for Max to face what he'd been running from all along. The silence between them wasn't awkward or uncomfortable—it was purposeful, like the calm before a storm.

Max could feel Eli's eyes on him, waiting, as if the man knew where Max's thoughts were headed before Max did.

There was something unnerving about it, like Eli could see through every defense Max had built, every layer of guilt and regret. But instead of being repelled by it, Max found himself oddly comforted by Eli's presence. It was as if Eli understood something that Max hadn't yet grasped.

The truck rolled along the road, the night thick and impenetrable around them. The faint whine of the engine was the only sound, apart from the occasional gust of wind rattling the windows. Every mile they drove felt like another step into the past, into memories that Max wasn't ready to revisit. The air inside the truck seemed to grow heavier with each passing moment, thick with the weight of things left unsaid.

Without warning, Eli spoke, his voice cutting through the thick air. "You ever think about where it all started?"

Max blinked, his chest tightening. "What do you mean?"

Eli didn't look at him. His eyes were focused on the road ahead, but Max could feel the weight of his words. "You and Eve. Where did it begin for you? Not the end, but the beginning."

The beginning.

Max's grip tightened on the wheel. The beginning. His mind drifted back to the classroom, to the sun-dappled windows, the innocent laughter, and the quiet moments between him and Eve that had sparked something far deeper than friendship. It was a time before the pain, before the mistakes, when everything seemed possible, and the future was full of hope.

"It started with her smile," Max said softly, his voice barely a whisper. "That's all it took."

And just like that, the world around him faded. The road, the truck, even Eli—everything dissolved into the past, pulling Max back to where it all began.

***

Max sat at his desk, the familiar hum of the classroom filling the air around him. He was ten years old, awkward, shy, and hopelessly captivated by Eve, who sat a few desks away. Her smile—God, that smile—had always been his undoing. It was infectious, bright, and seemed to light up the whole room. Even on his worst days, that smile had a way of making the world feel a little less overwhelming, a little more bearable.

The room was bathed in golden light, the afternoon sun streaming through the tall windows, casting long shadows across the worn wooden floors. Outside, the sounds of kids playing filtered in, a distant echo of freedom. But for Max, the world had shrunk to this small space, to this moment where Eve's presence seemed to fill every corner of the room.

Mrs. Thomas droned on at the blackboard, talking about multiplication tables, but Max's attention was fixed on Eve. He couldn't help it. There was something about her, even then, that made him feel like he was seeing the world for the first time. She was different from the other kids— brighter, kinder, with a light in her eyes that seemed to promise something better than the dull routine of everyday life.

And then, as if she could sense his gaze, Eve turned and caught his eye. Her smile widened, and Max felt his face flush with embarrassment. He quickly looked down at his notebook, pretending to be interested in the numbers scribbled there. His heart raced, thudding against his ribs like a drum. He felt like he'd been caught doing something he shouldn't, even though all he had done was look at her.

"Maxwell Hamblen!" Mrs. Thomas's voice cut through his thoughts, snapping him back to the present. "What's 172 times 6?"

Max blinked, his mind scrambling. He had no idea. His face flushed red as the rest of the class giggled. But before he could stammer out an answer, Mrs. Thomas added, "Or is Eve teaching the class today?"

The room erupted in soft laughter, and Max felt like he wanted to disappear. But when he looked back at Eve, she wasn't laughing at him. She was smiling, a warm, encouraging smile that seemed to tell him it was okay. That he didn't have to be embarrassed.

It was in that moment, with the sunlight casting her in a warm glow and the teasing laughter of his classmates fading into the background, that Max felt it for the first time—an undeniable pull toward her, a sense of connection that went beyond words or explanations. She wasn't just another classmate. She was someone who saw him, really saw him, in a way no one else did.

Max felt a warmth spread through him, a quiet sense of belonging that he hadn't realized he'd been missing. He didn't know it then, but that was the moment everything had begun. The moment he realized that Eve wasn't just another classmate. She was someone special. Someone he wanted to be around, even if he didn't quite understand why yet.

Max blinked, the memory fading, dissolving into the present. His chest felt tight, and for a moment, he had forgotten where he was. Forgotten that Eve was gone, and that the classroom was a world he could never return to. The weight of that realization settled over him like a thick blanket, suffocating and heavy.

"That was the first time," Max said quietly, his voice barely audible. "The first time I knew."

Eli didn't respond right away. He let the silence stretch, as if giving Max the space to sit with the memory, to feel it in his bones. There was a weight to Eli's silence, a kind of respect that Max hadn't expected. Eli wasn't pushing him, wasn't demanding answers or explanations. He was just… there. Waiting.

Then, softly, Eli asked, "And what did you do with that?"

Max swallowed hard, his throat tight. "I spent the rest of my life trying to protect her. Trying to keep her safe."

Eli nodded, his expression unreadable. "But what about the times she protected you?"

Max's breath caught in his throat. He hadn't thought about it like that. He had always seen himself as the one who had to protect Eve, to keep her from harm. But there were moments—so many moments—where it had been Eve who had saved him. From himself. From his own doubts. From the world.

***

They were teenagers now, sitting under the old oak tree behind St. Joseph's Catholic School. The summer air was warm, the sky a perfect, cloudless blue. Max sat with his back against the tree, his legs stretched out in front of him, while Eve lay on her back beside him, staring up at the sky.

The branches of the tree stretched wide above them, casting dappled shadows across the grass. The smell of summer—fresh cut grass, sun-warmed earth—filled the air. It was the kind of day that felt endless, like time itself had slowed down just for them.

"I wish summer never ended," Eve said, her voice soft and wistful.

Max turned to look at her, his heart heavy with unspoken words. He knew what she meant. Summer was their time. It was when they could escape the small town they both hated, when they could dream about a future that felt just out of reach.

"Yeah," Max said quietly. "Me too."

But even as he said the words, he could feel the tension building in his chest. Eve had dreams—big dreams. Dreams that involved leaving, moving away, starting a new life somewhere far from here. And Max… Max wasn't sure he could follow her.

He loved her. God, he loved her more than anything. But the thought of her leaving terrified him. He wanted to be with her, to protect her, to build a life together. But what if that wasn't what she wanted?

"What are you thinking about?" Eve asked, turning her head to look at him.

Max hesitated, unsure of how to put his feelings into words. "I don't know," he said finally. "The future, I guess."

Eve smiled, reaching out to take his hand. "The future's going to be amazing, Max. You'll see."

And in that moment, Max believed her. Because she had always been the one to see the possibilities, to believe in things he couldn't. She had always been the one to make him feel like maybe, just maybe, they could make it through anything.

The memory faded, and Max was back in the truck, his heart heavy with the weight of what could have been.

"You were always trying to protect her," Eli said quietly. "But maybe she was the one who was protecting you."

Max swallowed hard, his throat tight with emotion. He didn't know what to say. He had spent so long carrying the guilt of not being able to save her, of not being enough. But maybe, just maybe, Eli was right. Maybe Eve had always been the one saving him, shielding him from the weight of his own doubts, his own failures.

"I never saw it like that," Max admitted, his voice barely above a whisper. His eyes were fixed on the road ahead, but his mind was far away, lost in the echoes of a life that felt like it had slipped through his fingers. "I always thought it was my job to protect her. To be the one who fixed everything."

Eli's gaze softened, his voice gentle. "Maybe that's where you got it wrong, Max. She didn't need you to fix things. She just needed you to be there."

Max's chest tightened, the weight of those words settling over him like a heavy fog. How many times had Eve told him that? How many times had she tried to get him to slow down, to stop trying to fix everything and just be present with her? And how many times had he ignored it, convinced that the only way to show his love was by fixing, by solving, by taking control?

"Maybe I was trying to fix myself," Max said, the realization cutting through him like a knife. "Maybe I was trying to fix everything because I couldn't fix me."

Eli didn't respond immediately. He let the words hang in the air, giving them space to breathe, to sink in. Max could feel the truth of it, the way it gnawed at the edges of his heart, threatening to unravel everything he had built to protect himself.

"You can't fix what's already gone," Eli said softly. "But you can stop running from it."

Max's breath hitched in his throat, his grip on the steering wheel tightening. He had been running for so long—

running from the truth, from the pain, from the guilt. And now, sitting in the cab of this old truck, with Eli beside him and the night pressing in on all sides, he realized something he hadn't allowed himself to admit.

He was tired of running.

Max's eyes flicked to the rearview mirror, half expecting to see the ghosts of his past chasing after him. But there was nothing there—just the empty road stretching out behind them, dark and quiet. He had spent so much of his life looking back, haunted by the things he couldn't change, that he had forgotten how to look ahead.

"I don't know how to stop," Max admitted, his voice small, vulnerable. "I don't know how to let go."

Eli turned to him, his gaze steady, unwavering. "You don't have to do it all at once. You just have to take the first step."

Max swallowed hard, his throat tight with emotion. He didn't know if he was ready to take that step. Didn't know if he was ready to face the truth that had been lurking in the shadows for so long. But as the truck rumbled on, the road stretching out endlessly before them, he knew one thing for certain.

He couldn't keep running.

Not anymore.

Max let out a long, shaky breath, his chest tight with the weight of everything he had been carrying. The silence between them was thick, but it wasn't uncomfortable. It was the kind of silence that comes after a storm, when the air is heavy with the promise of something new, something unknown.

"I'm scared," Max admitted, his voice barely above a whisper.

Eli nodded, his expression soft. "I know. But you're not alone in this."

Max turned to look at him, his heart pounding in his chest. There was something in Eli's gaze—something deep and unspoken, something that made Max feel like maybe, just maybe, he didn't have to carry this burden alone.

For the first time in a long time, Max allowed himself to hope. It wasn't a big hope, not the kind that promised everything would be okay. But it was enough. Enough to make him believe that maybe there was a way out of the darkness. A way to stop running. A way to let go.

And as they drove on, the weight of memory pressing down on him, Max knew that whatever lay ahead, he would face it.

135

Because for the first time, he wasn't running away.

He was ready to face what lay beneath.

Chapter 15: The Foundation of Friendship

Max's thoughts drift as Eli's quiet question hangs in the air, drawing him back into memories he hadn't visited in years. Eli's voice cuts through the desert air, steady but probing: "When did you know she was the one?"

Max stares at the road, but his mind is miles away, years back, where his world had once felt hopeful and full of possibility. It wasn't just that he knew she was the one; it was that she had always been there, like a constant force—like gravity.

He could still remember the first time they had met—years before they were even teenagers—how she had marched up to him on the playground, hands on her hips, and demanded to know why he always sat by himself. Max had been a quiet kid back then, content to observe the world from a distance, but Eve had never been one to let anyone remain on the sidelines. She had plopped down beside him, all smiles and confidence, and from that moment on, they had been inseparable.

As they grew up, their friendship had deepened in ways Max hadn't fully understood at the time. There was an ease to their connection, like they had known each other in another life. By the time they hit high school, Max had taken for granted that she would always be there—her laughter, her relentless optimism, her ability to make the world feel less daunting.

Max was sixteen when he first realized how much Eve had become woven into the fabric of his life. They had spent hours in each other's company by then, but it wasn't until the day of the school talent show that he felt it—something more than just camaraderie.

He had been backstage, waiting to perform his piece, heart hammering in his chest, unsure of himself. Max wasn't exactly the outgoing type, and the idea of standing on stage, playing guitar in front of his entire school, had nearly made him back out. But Eve had been there, right from the beginning, telling him he'd be great, that he could do anything if he just let himself try.

Eve wasn't in the show, but she had been there in the crowd, rooting for him with that wide smile of hers. She had sat in the front row, always supportive, always making him feel like he wasn't alone. It was like her presence had been the only thing holding him together in those moments before he stepped out onto the stage.

Back then, she had been a force of nature—always laughing, always cheering for her friends. But it wasn't until that night, when he fumbled through his guitar solo, that he realized how much her opinion mattered. When the lights came up and the applause started, Max's eyes had gone straight to her, searching her face before anyone else's. Her smile had been warm, proud, like she had known all along that he would do just fine.

Max had felt his heart catch in his throat. The applause was for him, but all he cared about was that look in Eve's eyes—that reassurance, that unwavering belief in him. That was the moment he realized he needed her in his life in a way that went far beyond friendship.

After the show, when everyone else had crowded around, congratulating him, Max had barely heard them. All he had wanted to do was find Eve, to hear what she thought, to know if he had made her proud. And when she finally reached him, pushing through the crowd with that easy grin, all Max could think was how lucky he was to have her in his life.

"You were amazing!" she had said, pulling him into a hug that felt like home. "I knew you could do it."

Max had stood there, frozen, her arms wrapped around him, his heart racing like he was still on stage. It was the first time he had really noticed the way her touch lingered, the way her laughter seemed to sink into his skin and stay there.

He never said it out loud, but that was the moment he realized that Eve wasn't just his best friend. She was his anchor. They spent every moment they could together after that—talking on the phone late into the night, or meeting up to hang out under the tree, sharing secrets and making each other laugh.

She wasn't just the girl next door; she was the one who knew him better than anyone. They had their own shorthand, their own private jokes, and he always felt like the best version of himself when she was around. For years, their relationship had remained easy, uncomplicated, a friendship that felt like home. He hadn't wanted to push for more, hadn't even thought he needed more.

But everything had changed as they grew older, as the world around them began to shift. Max remembered the afternoons they spent together at the football games—Eve with her cheerleading squad, him in the stands, secretly hoping she'd glance up at him between cheers. The football players, especially Steve Sommers, the star quarterback, always hovered near her, flashing their confident smiles. Max couldn't compete with Steve's easy charm or his star status, but it never seemed to matter.

The memory of those games lingered in Max's mind, sharp and bittersweet. He had sat there, watching her, feeling like an outsider in his own life. Steve had been everything Max wasn't—popular, outgoing, the kind of guy who could have any girl he wanted. And yet, when the games ended, it wasn't Steve Sommers who Eve was walking to her car with—it was Max.

They'd go grab burgers at the diner, sit in a booth until it was late, talking about everything and nothing. Eve would lean across the table, eyes sparkling with mischief, and Max would feel like he was the luckiest guy in the world—just being her friend was enough.

Until it wasn't.

He had never told her, not back then. He had buried his feelings so deep, believing that their friendship was enough, that wanting more would ruin everything. But it was in those years—before they had ever even thought about dating—that Max realized Eve wasn't just a friend. She was his world, long before he'd ever worked up the courage to admit it.

He remembered the day they skipped class, heading out to the park instead, lying on the grass beneath the old oak tree they had claimed as their own. Eve had been talking about her dreams of leaving their small town, of moving to the city, of becoming something bigger than what this place could offer.

Max had listened, nodding along, but inside, all he could think about was how empty his life would be if she wasn't in it. The thought of her leaving—of her going off to chase her dreams without him—had terrified him in a way he hadn't been able to explain. He had smiled and encouraged her, told her she could do anything, but deep down, he had been scared. Scared that one day, she would realize she didn't need him anymore.

"Did you ever think you'd lose her?" Eli's voice broke through the memory, pulling Max back to the present.

Max's breath caught in his throat, and he blinked, shaking off the memory. Lose her? The thought had never even crossed his mind back then. Not until the world started to crumble.

"I didn't think I could lose her," Max admitted, his voice thick with emotion. "She was always there, always a part of my life. I didn't know how to imagine a world without her."

Eli's gaze stayed fixed on the road ahead, but his words were soft, measured. "It's funny, isn't it? How we never realize how much we have until we're faced with losing it."

Max nodded, swallowing hard. "I never thought about it. Not until it was too late."

His mind flashed back to the last conversation they had before Eve got sick. It had been a normal day, one of those afternoons where they had gone for a drive with no destination in mind, just enjoying each other's company. They had talked about everything, from silly jokes to the future. And Max had taken it all for granted—every word, every laugh, every moment.

He hadn't known that day would be the last time their lives would feel normal. He hadn't known that within a few short months, everything would change—that the easy laughter would be replaced with hospital visits, that the future they had always talked about would slip through their fingers like sand.

The weight of it all settled heavily on Max's chest. He had never let himself think about those early days, when everything between him and Eve had been simple and unburdened by the future. But now, sitting in the truck with Eli beside him, it all came rushing back—the missed opportunities, the words he hadn't said, the feelings he had kept hidden.

"She was my best friend," Max whispered, more to himself than to Eli. "And I never told her how much she meant to me. Not until it was almost too late."

Eli didn't respond right away. He let the silence stretch, giving Max the space to feel the weight of his own words. When he finally spoke, his voice was quiet but firm. "It's never too late to say what needs to be said, Max. Not if you're still here to say it."

Max's chest tightened. He didn't know if that was true anymore. Maybe it had been too late, even before Eve got sick. Maybe he had waited too long to tell her how much she meant to him—how she had been the foundation of his life, long before they had ever realized it themselves.

As the truck rumbled on, the road stretching endlessly ahead of them, Max couldn't shake the feeling that he had spent his entire life trying to make up for the things he hadn't said. He had built his world around Eve, and when she had been taken from him, it had felt like everything had crumbled. But maybe, just maybe, there was still time to rebuild.

145

Max let out a long, shaky breath, his mind swirling with memories of the life he had built with Eve—memories of friendship, of laughter, of love. The road ahead felt uncertain, but for the first time, he was ready to face it. Ready to stop running.

Chapter 16: The Spark of Something More

Max hadn't thought about it in years. The moment their friendship shifted, how fragile it had felt. He had buried it deep under the weight of everything that came after—Eve's illness, the choices he made, the life they had tried to build together. But now, sitting in the truck with Eli's quiet presence beside him, those old memories started to resurface.

It wasn't just that their relationship had changed—it was the way it had happened. Subtle, like a current beneath the surface that had finally broken through. And it all began at one of Steve Sommers' games.

Eli's question had snapped Max out of his thoughts, pulling him back into a memory that felt both distant and immediate.

"When did you know things changed?"

He hadn't wanted to revisit that moment, but now it was all rushing back to him. It was during her cheerleading days, right before everything shifted between them. And it all began at one of Steve Sommers' football games.

It was the last game of their junior year, and the whole school was buzzing with excitement. Steve Sommers, the school's golden boy, was leading the team to yet another victory. Max had never cared much for the guy—always the center of attention, always getting what he wanted. Steve was the kind of person who didn't have to try; things just seemed to fall into place for him, whether it was winning a game or getting the attention of every girl in school.

Max sat in the stands, his usual spot away from the crowd, watching Eve with the cheerleading squad. He could feel the energy of the crowd buzzing around him, the roar of voices as the game hit its peak. The smell of popcorn and sweat mingled in the cool night air, and the bleachers vibrated beneath him as the fans stomped their feet in excitement.

Eve was radiant in her cheer uniform, her smile brighter than the stadium lights. Her laughter carried across the field, mingling with the cheers of the crowd. But while the other girls seemed caught up in the attention and the excitement of the game, Eve had always been different. She was grounded, down-to-earth, and no matter how much the crowd cheered or how many eyes were on her, she always stayed real.

Max watched as Steve made another touchdown, the crowd erupting into wild applause. The cheers filled the stadium, drowning out everything else, but Max's focus wasn't on the game—it was on Eve. She led the cheers with enthusiasm, her voice echoing across the field as she pumped her fists in the air. But every time the crowd quieted, Max noticed her eyes drifting toward him. Even with Steve basking in the glory of his latest victory, Max could tell—there was something between him and Eve that no amount of touchdowns could overshadow.

He had always known they had a special bond. But it was that night, watching her on the sidelines, that Max realized something had shifted between them. There was a spark, something unspoken, that had been there for years but had finally ignited.

The noise of the crowd faded into the background as Max's mind drifted. He could still remember the way his heart had pounded in his chest, the way the world seemed to narrow down to just him and Eve. He had sat there, alone in the stands, feeling like the world was about to change but not knowing how or why.

After the game, as the team was celebrated and Steve Sommers soaked in the adoration of the crowd, Max hung back. He had always kept his distance, content to watch from the sidelines, letting the noise and excitement swirl around him. He wasn't the type to seek the spotlight, and he had never felt the need to compete with guys like Steve. But that night, something felt different.

Max watched as Steve strutted toward Eve, flashing that grin that always seemed to work on everyone. Steve was the kind of guy who could have any girl he wanted, and Max had always assumed that eventually, Eve would fall for his charm like everyone else.

But not this time.

Eve glanced toward Max, her eyes searching the stands until they locked on his. Steve was talking, saying something Max couldn't hear, but Eve wasn't listening. Her focus was on Max, and in that moment, everything became clear.

When she finally pulled away from Steve and made her way over to Max, Max could feel the tension in the air. It wasn't just the crowd or the noise of the game—it was the weight of what had just happened. The shift between them had finally surfaced, and there was no turning back.

"You okay?" Eve asked, her voice soft amid the crowd's noise.

Max shrugged, trying to play it cool. "Yeah, just... watching."

She smiled, but it wasn't the same carefree smile she'd given the others. This one felt like it was just for him, like it held something more—something unspoken but undeniable.

"What did Steve want?" Max asked, trying to sound casual, though he could feel the weight of the question. He hated how jealous it made him feel, but he couldn't help it.

Eve shrugged, glancing back toward the field where Steve was still basking in the afterglow of the game. "He wanted to take me out tonight. But I'm not interested."

Max blinked, surprised. "You're not?"

She shook her head, her eyes locking with his. "No, I think I'd rather go grab a burger with you."

Max's heart skipped a beat, the words hanging in the air between them. For a moment, he wasn't sure if he had heard her right. She was turning down Steve Sommers— Steve Sommers, the golden boy of the school—to hang out with him?

And just like that, everything changed.

They walked away from the field, leaving Steve and the crowd behind, and for the first time, Max felt something more—a spark of something that had been there all along but had finally ignited. It was the beginning of them.

Max's hands tightened on the wheel, the memory fading but the warmth of it still lingering. They'd always had a bond, but that night, under the stadium lights, something shifted. It wasn't about Steve or the crowd. It was about them—what they had, what they'd always had. And for the first time, Max felt like maybe, just maybe, it wasn't crazy to think that Eve could want something more from him.

As they drove away from the stadium that night, sitting in the diner with their burgers and fries, everything felt different. The easy friendship they had shared for years was still there, but now there was something more—a new current running beneath the surface, one that neither of them could ignore. Every glance, every touch, felt charged with a new energy, like they were standing on the edge of something big, something neither of them was ready to name.

But even with that shift, there was still fear. Max had always been afraid of losing her—afraid that one day, someone like Steve would come along and sweep her off her feet. And for a long time, he had convinced himself that it was enough to just be her friend, to keep his feelings buried deep, where they couldn't complicate things.

But that night had changed everything. Max couldn't pretend anymore. He couldn't ignore the way his heart raced when she looked at him, the way her smile made the world feel right again. He didn't know what the future held for them, but he knew one thing for sure: he wasn't going to let someone like Steve take her away from him.

Eli broke the silence, his voice soft, cutting through Max's thoughts. "You didn't let him have her."

Max's jaw clenched, his grip tightening on the steering wheel. "No. I didn't."

He had fought for her, in his own quiet way. He hadn't been the loudest, the flashiest, or the most confident guy around. But he had been there for her, always, and that had been enough.

For a long time, he had wondered if she had seen him the same way—if she had ever felt that same spark he had carried for so long. And when she chose him over Steve, when she looked at him with those eyes that seemed to see right through him, he knew. He knew that what they had was real, and that it had been there all along, waiting for the right moment to surface.

Max's thoughts drifted as the truck hummed along the empty road. That night had been the beginning of something, but it had also marked the end of their innocence. After that, everything had changed. Their friendship had deepened, their bond growing stronger with every shared moment, every late-night conversation.

But it had also marked the beginning of the fear—fear of losing her, fear of not being enough, fear of the world crashing down around them.

Eli's voice cut through the quiet again, softer this time. "Did you ever tell her how you felt back then?"

Max hesitated, his mind racing. He hadn't, not really. Not until it was almost too late. He had always believed that actions spoke louder than words, that being there for her was enough. But now, looking back, he wondered if he had been wrong.

"No," Max finally admitted, his voice low. "I didn't."

Chapter 17: In the Rhythm of the Everyday

Max swallowed hard, the memories stirring as Eli's question echoed in his mind: "What was your happiest memory with her?"

There were so many to choose from, but one stood out, not because it was grand or monumental, but because it was simple—one of those moments that felt so full, so perfect, that it stayed with him even now, years later.

It was a normal day, nothing special. They had been engaged for a few months by then, and Max and Eve had fallen into the easy rhythm of spending time together, each day blending into the next. No more nervous stares, no more second-guessing. It was the kind of comfort Max had never known before—something that had become more precious with time.

That Saturday, they had spent the afternoon at the local flea market, wandering through rows of dusty antiques, old vinyl records, and trinkets that people no longer wanted. The flea market was one of Eve's favorite places. She loved the thrill of the hunt, sifting through the forgotten and discarded to find something that held meaning. Max had always admired that about her—how she could find beauty in the smallest things.

The air was filled with the scent of hot dogs and funnel cakes, the buzz of conversations blending with the occasional honk of a distant car. People moved between the stalls, chatting with vendors, their arms full of treasures waiting to be rediscovered. Max walked beside Eve, watching as her eyes lit up with each new find, her excitement contagious.

"This place is a gold mine," she said, her voice full of enthusiasm. She had already found a stack of old books that she insisted on bringing home, even though their apartment was already overflowing with her collection. Max didn't mind. He loved the way she got so absorbed in her discoveries, like she was piecing together a puzzle no one else could see.

Max chuckled as Eve darted toward a table filled with records, her fingers flipping through the stacks with practiced ease. He wasn't much of a music guy himself, but he had learned over the years that music was one of Eve's great loves. She could spend hours listening to albums, analyzing lyrics, getting lost in the melodies.

"This one," she said, pulling out an album with a worn cover. She held it up to Max, a bright smile lighting up her face. "I've been looking for this forever."

Max looked at the cover and raised an eyebrow. "Fleetwood Mac?"

Eve rolled her eyes playfully, her fingers tracing the edge of the album cover. "Don't give me that look. These songs are timeless." She clutched the record to her chest as if it were treasure. "We're getting this."

Max couldn't help but smile. He had no real opinion about Fleetwood Mac, but seeing Eve's excitement made him want to listen to every track with her. She had a way of making the ordinary feel extraordinary. "Alright, alright," Max said, pulling out his wallet. "You win."

Later that evening, they found themselves back at Eve's small apartment, the record spinning on her old turntable as they sat cross-legged on the floor. The scent of pizza lingered in the air, mingling with the sound of Stevie Nicks' voice filling the space between them. The windows were open, letting in the cool evening breeze, and outside, the city hummed with life—honking cars, distant chatter, the occasional bark of a dog. But inside, it was just them.

Max leaned back against the couch, a slice of pizza in one hand, watching Eve as she swayed to the music, her eyes closed, lost in the rhythm. There was something so effortless about her, something that made everything else fade away. She had this ability to make any moment feel like the best one yet, even if they were just sitting on the floor of her cramped apartment, surrounded by half-eaten pizza and empty soda bottles.

He couldn't remember a time he had felt more content. The world outside didn't matter. The future they had planned didn't matter. It was just them, in this moment, with the music and the warmth of their love filling the room.

Without a word, Eve reached out her hand to Max. He looked at her, surprised, as she beckoned him with that playful smile of hers.

"Dance with me," she said softly, her eyes sparkling with mischief.

Max hesitated for only a second before taking her hand. She pulled him to his feet, drawing him into a slow dance right there in the middle of her tiny living room. The pizza, the music, the flickering lights from the street outside —it was all so mundane, yet Max couldn't remember ever feeling so alive.

They moved together, swaying to the music, the soft sound of Stevie Nicks' voice the only thing breaking the quiet. Eve rested her head against his chest, and Max could feel her heartbeat, steady and strong, as if it were in sync with his own. He wrapped his arms around her, holding her close, feeling the warmth of her body against his. There was something so right about it, so perfect in its simplicity.

"I love this song," Eve whispered as they swayed, her head resting against his chest.

Max smiled, his heart swelling as he held her close. "Yeah, I know," he said softly.

It was one of those moments that felt timeless, like the world had slowed down just for them. Max closed his eyes, letting the music wash over him, letting himself get lost in the feeling of being with her. It wasn't about the future or the past. It wasn't about the plans they had made or the dreams they had shared. It was about now—about being with her, in this moment, in the rhythm of the everyday.

They danced like that for what felt like hours, moving in sync, their world reduced to the warmth between them and the music playing in the background. Max didn't need words to tell her how he felt. It was in the way he held her, in the way he moved with her, in the way he breathed her in.

As the song faded into the next track, Eve lifted her head and smiled up at him, her eyes full of love and something deeper—something that made Max feel like he could take on the world as long as she was by his side.

"What are you thinking about?" she asked, her voice soft and curious.

Max shrugged, his voice barely above a whisper. "Just… how lucky I am."

Eve's smile widened, and she stood on her tiptoes, pressing a kiss to his cheek. "You're not the only one," she whispered.

That night had been so ordinary, yet so full. It wasn't about the grand gestures or the big moments. It was about the little things—the way they laughed together, the way they moved together, the way they understood each other without having to say anything. It was in the rhythm of the everyday that Max had found his happiness.

As Max drove through the desert, the memory of that night lingered, warm and bittersweet. He hadn't realized it then, but that simple night in Eve's apartment had been one of the happiest moments of his life. It wasn't about the future they had planned. It wasn't about the dreams they had shared. It was about being with her, in that moment, in the here and now.

But now, all he had left were those memories—those quiet moments that he couldn't get back.

Eli's voice broke through the silence, pulling Max out of his thoughts. "But then it all started slipping, didn't it?"

Max exhaled slowly, gripping the steering wheel tighter. "Yeah. It did."

He could still remember how the weight of the world had started to press down on them, how the rhythm of their everyday lives had shifted into something more uncertain, more fragile. It had started with the small things—the doctor's appointments, the missed calls, the quiet conversations that turned into long silences. Max had tried to hold onto those happy moments, tried to keep their life together, but it had slipped through his fingers like sand.

"Why do you think it changed?" Eli asked, his voice soft but probing.

Max swallowed hard, his chest tightening. He didn't have an answer. Or maybe he did, but he wasn't ready to face it yet. "I don't know," he admitted, his voice rough with emotion. "Maybe I wasn't enough."

Eli didn't respond right away. He let the silence stretch, giving Max the space to sit with his thoughts, to feel the weight of his own words. When he finally spoke, his voice was steady, almost gentle. "Maybe it wasn't about being enough, Max. Maybe it was just about being there."

Max's chest tightened, the weight of those words settling over him like a heavy blanket. How many times had Eve told him that? How many times had she tried to get him to just be with her, to stop trying to fix things, to stop trying to control the future?

"I tried," Max whispered, his voice thick with regret. "I really tried."

Eli nodded, his gaze steady. "I know."

But in the end, it hadn't been enough. The world had shifted, their lives had changed, and the rhythm of the everyday had been replaced with something else—something darker, something harder to bear.

As the truck rumbled on through the desert night, Max felt the weight of those memories pressing down on him, but for the first time, he wasn't running from them. He was sitting with them, letting them wash over him, letting himself feel the loss, the regret, the love that had defined his life with Eve.

Chapter 18: A Perfect Day

The desert stretched endlessly before them, but Max's mind was elsewhere, lost in the warmth of a memory that felt like a summer breeze. Eli's voice cut through the silence once again, gentle but insistent: "What was another of your best days together?"

Max smiled to himself. So many memories came rushing back, but there was one that stood out—a day that had been full of laughter, sunshine, and the promise of endless tomorrows.

It had been a spontaneous trip—something Eve had insisted on. "We need a break from everything," she had said, flashing that mischievous grin that always made Max's heart skip a beat. Before he knew it, they were driving out of town, heading for the coast with no real plan, just the open road and each other.

Max had always been a planner, someone who needed to know every step of the journey. But with Eve, life never went according to plan, and that was what he loved most about her. She had a way of pulling him out of his comfort zone, of reminding him that sometimes the best moments were the ones you couldn't plan for. The ones that happened when you just let go.

They ended up in a little beachside town, the kind you saw in postcards—small shops lining the boardwalk, the salty air thick with the sound of crashing waves. The town had a timeless quality to it, like it had been untouched by the rush of the modern world. Everything seemed to move a little slower there, like the ocean itself was dictating the pace of life.

The air was thick with the smell of salt and sunscreen, the breeze carrying with it the sound of distant laughter and the faint calls of seagulls overhead. Max felt a sense of peace settle over him as they wandered through the town, hand in hand, without any real destination in mind. For the first time in what felt like forever, the weight of the world had lifted, and all that mattered was the moment they were in.

They spent the day exploring, wandering through the small, quirky shops that lined the boardwalk. Eve's eyes lit up at every little discovery—a vintage postcard here, an old photograph there. Max could see the joy in her eyes as she found a small treasure in each store they entered. She had a way of finding beauty in the simplest things, and it was one of the things that had drawn Max to her in the first place.

At one point, they had stopped at a small café on the corner of the boardwalk, the kind of place where the tables were mismatched, and the menu was written in chalk on the wall. They sat outside, sipping iced coffee and people-watching as the world moved around them. Max remembered the way Eve had leaned back in her chair, sunglasses perched on her nose, a satisfied smile on her lips.

"I could get used to this," she had said, her voice full of contentment.

Max had smiled back, watching her, his heart swelling with love. "Me too," he had said, meaning it more than she could ever know.

As the day went on, they wandered down to the beach, their feet sinking into the warm sand as they walked along the shoreline. The sun was high in the sky, casting a golden glow over everything. The ocean stretched out before them, vast and endless, the sound of the waves crashing against the shore a constant rhythm that seemed to sync with their footsteps.

They had found a quiet spot away from the crowds, spreading out a blanket and settling in for the afternoon. Eve had brought a book, but she barely touched it, preferring instead to lie back and watch the waves roll in and out. Max remembered how peaceful she had looked, her eyes closed, her face turned toward the sun, as if she was soaking in every bit of warmth and light.

At some point, they had started talking—about life, about their future, about all the things they wanted to do together. It wasn't a serious conversation, more like a playful daydream of what their life could be. Eve had always been the dreamer, the one who saw endless possibilities, while Max had been the one to keep them grounded. But on that day, with the sun and the sand and the ocean surrounding them, Max had allowed himself to dream with her.

"I want to travel," Eve had said, her voice full of excitement. "I want to see everything—the mountains, the cities, the deserts. All of it."

Max had smiled, watching her eyes light up as she spoke. "We will," he had promised, even though he wasn't sure how or when. "We'll go everywhere you want."

Eve had laughed then, a sound so full of joy that it had made Max's heart ache in the best way. "You always know what to say," she had teased, poking him playfully in the side.

They had spent the rest of the afternoon like that—talking, laughing, letting the world fall away. At some point, Eve had gotten up and wandered down to the water, her feet sinking into the wet sand as the waves lapped at her ankles. Max had watched her from the blanket, a smile tugging at his lips as she twirled in the shallow water, her hair catching the breeze.

"I could stay here forever," she had said, her voice soft, her eyes on the horizon.

Max had smiled, the words coming easily. "Me too."

It was one of those days that felt perfect—like nothing could touch them, like the future was bright and endless, stretching out before them just as the ocean did. They had been so full of hope back then, so sure that their life together would be filled with days like that one. Max hadn't known it at the time, but that day would become one of the memories he would hold onto when everything else started to fall apart.

As the sun began to set, casting a warm golden glow over the water, Eve had pulled Max close, her arms wrapped around his waist. "This is one of those days," she had said, her voice soft against the backdrop of the waves. "One of those days we'll remember forever."

Max had kissed her then, feeling the weight of her words, the truth of them sinking deep into his heart. He hadn't known it at the time, but she had been right. That day, so simple and perfect, had become one of those memories he would carry with him, even when everything else began to fall apart.

As the sun dipped below the horizon, painting the sky in shades of orange and pink, they had made their way back to the car, their hands still intertwined, the day lingering in their hearts like a promise. Max remembered the drive back home, the way Eve had leaned her head against the window, her eyes closed, a small smile on her lips. He had watched her, feeling an overwhelming sense of love and gratitude for the life they were building together.

But like all perfect days, it had ended. And soon, the weight of the world had come crashing back in.

Max blinked, the memory fading like the last rays of sunlight dipping below the horizon. The smile lingered on his lips, though, the warmth of that day still alive inside him. It had been perfect—a moment of pure joy, untouched by the darkness that would come later.

Eli's voice broke through, quiet and thoughtful. "It's funny how the best memories always seem to come before everything changes."

Max's smile faltered, the weight of Eli's words settling over him like a cold shadow. He knew where the memory was leading—back to a time when everything had started to unravel. Back to that night with Eve's father.

Max's grip on the steering wheel tightened as the memory of that night came rushing back. He could feel it creeping up on him, the tension, the fear, the way everything had spiraled out of control. It had been the beginning of the end, though he hadn't known it at the time.

"Yeah," he whispered, his voice strained. "Everything changed after that."

Chapter 19: The Night of the Dress

Max's thoughts drifted back to a night that had shaped so much of his connection with Eve, another night when he realized just how deep his feelings for her truly went. He had always been protective, but that night had shown him just how far he was willing to go for her. It wasn't just about love; it was about standing up for someone when they needed it most, when the world seemed intent on tearing them down.

The memory of that night always returned to him in fragments—moments that had seared themselves into his mind. He had tried to forget the hurt on Eve's face, the cold anger in her father's eyes, but some things refused to fade, no matter how much time passed.

***

It was their senior year, a time that was supposed to be filled with excitement and anticipation for the future. But for Eve, home life had always been tense. Her father was a man who demanded control, whose temper simmered just below the surface, and any spark could set him off. That night, Max had been at her house, sitting at the kitchen table while Eve excitedly showed her mother a catalog of prom dresses. Her eyes sparkled as she pointed to one dress in particular, a soft lavender gown that made her face light up.

"I love this one, Mom. It's perfect, isn't it?" she asked, her voice filled with the hope that this prom might be a bright spot in a difficult year.

For a brief moment, Eve's mother had smiled, her face softening as she looked at the dress. Max had seen that glimmer of maternal affection, the brief hint that maybe, just maybe, this would be a moment of peace for Eve. He had always sensed the tension in this house, the unspoken rules that dictated every conversation. Eve's mother had long since learned to keep quiet, to play along, to keep the peace. But tonight, for a moment, it seemed like things might be different.

Then the kitchen door swung open with force. The atmosphere changed instantly, as if the very air in the room had been sucked out. Eve's father stormed in, his face set in a deep scowl. He was a hard man, his anger often just below the surface, and tonight was no different. The sight of the catalog in Eve's hands only seemed to ignite his fury.

"You think I'm spending good money on that garbage? No way in hell!" he bellowed, crossing the room in long strides. His hand shot out, grabbing the catalog from Eve's hands and tearing it in half. The pages fluttered to the ground like fallen leaves, scattered across the worn floor.

Eve's face crumpled, her dreams of prom night shattering in an instant. Max could see the exact moment her hope dissolved—the way her eyes lost their light, the way her shoulders slumped as though the weight of the world had suddenly become unbearable. Tears welled up in her eyes, but she didn't cry. Not yet. She stood frozen, caught between her father's rage and the desire to stand her ground.

Max felt his chest tighten, a fiery heat rising in him. He couldn't sit back and watch this. He had seen Eve's father lash out before, his temper unpredictable and cruel, but tonight, something inside Max snapped. It wasn't just about the dress; it was about everything her father had taken from her over the years—the freedom, the joy, the ability to dream without fear. Without thinking, Max stood up, his chair scraping loudly against the floor. His blood boiled as he crossed the room in a few quick strides, placing himself between Eve and her father.

"You don't have to talk to her like that," Max said, his voice low but firm. He could feel the adrenaline pumping through his veins, his heart pounding in his chest. He had never confronted her father like this before, but tonight, he couldn't stay silent.

Eve's father's eyes flicked to Max, narrowing as he registered the challenge. For a moment, there was silence, the air in the room thick with tension. Max could see the way her father's jaw clenched, the muscles in his neck tightening. He wasn't used to being questioned, especially not by someone like Max—a boy, an outsider in his home.

"What did you say?" her father growled, stepping closer, his fists clenched at his sides. His face was twisted with anger, his eyes flashing with a kind of fury that sent a chill down Max's spine. But Max didn't back down. He couldn't. Not now.

"I said you don't have to treat her like this," Max repeated, his voice stronger now. "She just wants to go to prom. She deserves that."

Her father let out a bitter laugh, the sound cold and harsh. "You think you know what she deserves?" he spat, his voice dripping with disdain. "You think you can come into my house and tell me how to raise my daughter?"

Max's hands trembled with the effort to keep himself in check, to stop himself from doing something he might regret. "It's not about raising her," he said through gritted teeth. "It's about respecting her. She deserves better than this."

Eve's father took another step forward, his chest heaving with anger. Max could feel the tension rising, could sense that things were about to spiral out of control. His heart raced as he glanced at Eve, standing behind him, her eyes wide with fear and sadness. He wanted to protect her, to shield her from this, but he also knew that one wrong move could make things worse.

But then something happened—something Max hadn't expected. Eve's voice cut through the tension, soft but strong. "Dad, please," she said, her voice steady despite the tears brimming in her eyes. "Just stop."

Her father paused, his anger faltering for a moment as he looked at her. There was something in her voice, in the way she stood there, that seemed to break through the rage—if only for a second.

But the moment passed quickly, and her father's face hardened again. He turned his back on them, muttering under his breath as he stormed out of the kitchen, slamming the door behind him. The sound echoed through the house, the final punctuation to the confrontation that had left the air heavy with unresolved tension.

For a moment, there was silence. Max stood there, his chest heaving, his fists still clenched at his sides. He could feel the adrenaline slowly draining away, leaving him shaky and exhausted. Eve's mother remained where she was, her gaze fixed on the floor, her hands wringing together in her lap. She didn't say a word.

Max turned to Eve, his expression softening as he reached for her hand. "Let's go," he said quietly.

Eve nodded, her face pale and her eyes still filled with unshed tears. She didn't say anything as they left the house, stepping into the cool night air. The sky above them was dark and endless, a stark contrast to the suffocating atmosphere they had just escaped. The silence between them was heavy, but it wasn't uncomfortable. It was the kind of silence that comes after a storm, when the air is thick with the aftermath but also a sense of relief.

They walked down the driveway, the gravel crunching beneath their feet, neither of them speaking. Max could feel the weight of Eve's sorrow, and it broke his heart. He wanted to take it away, to shield her from it, but he knew that wasn't possible. All he could do was stand by her side, as he had always done.

As they reached his car, Eve finally spoke, her voice barely above a whisper. "Thank you."

Max turned to her, his heart aching at the sight of her tear-streaked face. "You don't have to thank me," he said softly. "I'm always going to be here for you, Eve. You know that."

Eve nodded, a small, sad smile tugging at her lips. "I know," she whispered, and for a moment, the weight of the world seemed to lift, if only slightly.

Later that Week: A Promise Fulfilled

A few days later, Max stood outside Eve's house, a garment bag in his hand and nervous energy coursing through him. He had spent the past several days working extra shifts, scrimping and saving every last dollar he could. He knew how much that dress had meant to her, and even though they hadn't spoken much since the night of the fight, he had made a decision. He was going to give her something no one else could—a moment of happiness, a piece of the life she deserved.

When Eve opened the door, her eyes were still rimmed with the sadness that had lingered since that night. Her smile had faded, replaced by a quiet resignation that made Max's chest ache. But when she saw the bag in his hand, her brow furrowed in confusion.

"What's that?" she asked, her voice hesitant, as though she was afraid to hope.

Max smiled, his heart swelling with the thought of seeing her happy again. "I got you something," he said softly, holding the bag out to her.

Eve took the bag slowly, her hands trembling as she unzipped it. Her eyes widened as she pulled the lavender dress from its protective cover, the very one she had wanted from the catalog. For a moment, she just stared at it, her breath catching in her throat.

"Max... how did you...?" she whispered, her voice breaking with emotion.

"I just... I couldn't stand seeing you upset," he admitted, his own voice thick with feeling. "You deserve this, Eve. You deserve to have one thing go right."

Eve's tears spilled over, but this time, they were tears of gratitude, of joy. She threw her arms around Max, holding him tightly as sobs wracked her body. The weight of her father's cruelty seemed to melt away in that moment, replaced by the warmth of Max's love.

"You didn't have to do this," she whispered into his chest, her voice barely audible. "You always do so much…"

Max stroked her hair gently, his heart aching at how much she had endured, how much she had been forced to grow up too soon. "I'd do anything for you, Eve. You know that."

In that moment, Max realized that he wasn't just standing up to her father. He was standing up for her, for the life they both dreamed of having together. And in doing so, he was making an unspoken promise—a promise that he would always be there for her, no matter how difficult things became.

The memory faded, and Max blinked, the weight of that night still heavy in his chest. He had been protecting Eve for as long as he could remember, always trying to shield her from the pain she didn't deserve. And now, even in the midst of everything that had gone wrong, that instinct to protect, to fix, had never left him.

Eli glanced at him, sensing the shift in Max's mood. "You've always been trying to protect her, haven't you?" Eli's voice was quiet but firm.

Max nodded, his throat tightening. "Yeah. I promised her I would."

Eli's gaze softened. "But you can't always be the one to save her, Max. Sometimes… it's about letting go."

Chapter 20: Promises Made

The weight of the past clung to Max like a heavy blanket, suffocating him as he navigated the winding road ahead. The air inside the truck felt thick, as if the memories Eli was pulling from him had a tangible presence. Every time Max thought he could catch his breath, another moment from his past crept in, reminding him of what he'd lost—and what he'd promised.

Eli, quiet and composed as ever, remained beside him, but it was clear that he was leading Max down a path he couldn't turn away from. The man's presence had become like the air itself—inescapable, his words echoing in the space between them.

"You've always been good at making promises, haven't you, Max?" Eli's voice was soft but sharp, cutting through the fog of memories swirling in Max's mind.

Max flinched slightly. He knew where this was heading. "Yeah," he muttered. "But keeping them… that's a different story."

"Is it?" Eli asked, his gaze unrelenting. "Maybe the problem wasn't in keeping them. Maybe it was in the promises themselves."

Max frowned, his chest tightening as Eli's words sank in. He didn't know how to respond. He had made so many promises—promises to Eve, promises to himself. Promises that, no matter how hard he tried, he could never keep.

And there was one promise in particular that haunted him more than any other.

The one that had come on a night filled with hope and love —a night that should've been perfect. But now, it loomed over him like a shadow.

***

The night was quiet, the stars spread across the sky like diamonds against a velvet backdrop. The air was crisp but held the warmth of spring, a hint of summer teasing the edges. Max sat in the front seat of his pickup truck, parked at the edge of an overlook that gave them a view of the small town below. It was their secret spot, a place they'd come to when they wanted to escape everything—school, family, the future that felt like a storm just over the horizon.

Max had parked the truck just as the last of the day's warmth clung to the earth, the fading sunlight casting long shadows over the trees. He could feel the quiet calm of the evening settling over them, the way the world seemed to slow down when they were together. It was the kind of night that felt like it belonged to them, like no one else existed except for him and Eve.

Beside him, Eve was radiant in her prom dress, a soft lavender gown that seemed to shimmer in the moonlight. Her hair fell in loose waves around her shoulders, and she wore a delicate silver necklace that caught the light when she moved. Her smile, though, was what took Max's breath away. It was the kind of smile that made everything else fade into the background, a smile that told him she was happy—really happy—in that moment.

Max had seen her in that dress earlier at the dance, surrounded by friends and laughter, the music pounding in the background. But it was here, in the quiet of the night, that he felt her presence most profoundly. She was more than beautiful—she was everything he had ever wanted, everything he had ever dreamed of. And tonight, he was going to make sure she knew that.

She looked at him, her eyes shining with curiosity and something deeper. "What's on your mind?" she asked softly, her voice cutting through the quiet night.

Max's heart pounded in his chest. He had been thinking about this moment for weeks, planning every detail, but now that it was here, he felt a weight settle in his stomach. His hands trembled slightly as he reached into his jacket pocket, his fingers brushing against the small velvet box he had kept hidden for weeks.

This was it.

He had always known that Eve was the one. From the moment he had seen her smile across the classroom, he had known. And tonight, standing on the edge of their future, he wanted to make sure she knew it too.

But as he touched the box, a wave of doubt washed over him. What if this wasn't the right time? What if he wasn't enough? Max had always tried to be strong for Eve, to be the one she could rely on. But deep down, he had always feared that he wasn't enough—that his love wouldn't be enough to protect her from the harshness of the world.

With a deep breath, Max pulled the box from his pocket and held it between them, his heart hammering against his ribcage. Eve's eyes widened, a soft gasp escaping her lips as she realized what was happening.

"Max…," she whispered, her voice full of emotion.

Max swallowed hard, his mouth suddenly dry. His hands shook as he opened the box, revealing the delicate engagement ring inside. It wasn't much—just a simple gold band with a small diamond set in the center. But it was his mother's ring, the one she had worn every day of her life, and it was the only thing of real value Max had left.

The ring held a special meaning for Max. His mother had worn it through the hardest times of her life—when she had received her health diagnosis, how she also had worked to hide her illness from max, how she had fought to keep their small family together. To Max, the ring wasn't just a piece of jewelry; it was a symbol of strength, of enduring love. And now, he was offering that same promise to Eve.

His voice was barely a whisper when he finally spoke. "Will you marry me?"

For a moment, time seemed to stand still. Max held his breath, his heart in his throat as he waited for Eve's answer. The world around them faded, the sounds of the night growing distant, and all he could see was her—those bright eyes, that smile, the way she looked at him like he was the only person who mattered.

And then, slowly, her lips curled into a smile. "Yes," she breathed, her voice trembling with emotion. "Of course I will."

Relief flooded through Max, his chest swelling with a joy so profound he thought he might burst. His hands still shook as he slid the ring onto her finger, but it fit perfectly, like it had always been meant for her.

Max leaned in, pressing his forehead against hers, their breaths mingling in the cool night air. "I promise," he whispered, his voice thick with emotion. "I promise I'll take care of you, Eve. I'll build us a home. I'll give you everything you've ever wanted. I'll never let anything happen to you."

Eve closed her eyes, her smile soft but full of understanding. "You don't have to promise me the world, Max," she said gently. "Just promise me you'll always be here. That's all I need."

Max nodded, his heart aching with the depth of his love for her. "I promise."

The memory faded, leaving Max breathless in the present. His hands tightened on the steering wheel, his knuckles swollen gripping the leather. That night had been perfect.

He had felt invincible, like nothing in the world could ever tear them apart.

But he had broken that promise. In the end, he hadn't been able to give Eve everything she had wanted. He hadn't been able to protect her from the one thing he couldn't control—her illness. And that failure had haunted him every day since.

Max could still see the way she had smiled at him that night, the way her eyes had lit up with hope and love. But now, that smile felt like a ghost, a reminder of the promises he had made and the ones he hadn't kept. He had wanted so desperately to protect her, to keep her safe, but in the end, he had been powerless.

"You made a lot of promises to her, didn't you?" Eli asked, his voice gentle but probing.

Max nodded, his throat tight. "Too many."

"And which ones did she need the most?"

Max swallowed hard, his heart heavy. "The ones I couldn't keep."

Eli's gaze was steady, unflinching. "Or the ones she didn't need you to keep."

Max frowned, confusion swirling in his chest. "What do you mean?"

"You promised her the world," Eli said quietly. "But maybe all she ever really needed was you. Not the promises. Not the house. Just you."

Max's chest tightened at those words, a familiar ache spreading through him. He had spent so long trying to build something for Eve, trying to give her the life she deserved. But in the end, maybe that hadn't been what she needed. Maybe all she had ever wanted was for him to be there, to be present with her in the moments that mattered.

"I thought I had to fix everything," Max whispered, his voice trembling. "I thought I had to make it all right."

Eli nodded. "But what if being there, truly being with her, was enough? What if that's all she needed?"

Max's vision blurred with unshed tears, the weight of Eli's words pressing down on him. He had spent so long punishing himself for not being able to save Eve, for not being able to keep his promises. But maybe—just maybe—

he had been enough. Maybe being there for her, loving her, had been all she had ever really needed.

"I don't know how to stop blaming myself," Max admitted, his voice thick with emotion.

Eli's gaze softened, and for a moment, Max saw something almost tender in his eyes. "You don't have to stop blaming yourself all at once. But maybe you can start by forgiving yourself. One promise at a time."

Max exhaled shakily, the truth of those words sinking in. Forgiving himself felt impossible. But for the first time, he could see a path forward, a way to begin letting go of the guilt that had been weighing him down for so long.

He wasn't ready yet. But he could try. And maybe that was enough.

Chapter 21: The Man Behind the Mask

The desert stretched endlessly ahead, but Max wasn't looking at the road. His mind was a storm of images and memories, each one louder than the last. He could feel the weight of Eli's gaze, steady and unyielding, but he kept his eyes fixed on the horizon. Eli hadn't spoken in a while, but Max could sense something coming.

"It's strange, isn't it?" Eli's voice cut through the silence like a blade. "How we never really know what someone else's day is going to look like. Take Mr. Davis, for example."

Max felt a chill running down his spine. He didn't want to think about Mr. Davis—not now, not ever. But Eli had a way of pulling thoughts to the surface, no matter how hard Max tried to bury them.

"What about him?" Max muttered, his voice rough.

Eli leaned back in his seat, his expression thoughtful. "Do you think Mr. Davis knew what was going to happen when he walked into the bank? Did you ever think that maybe, just maybe, he had plans for the weekend? Maybe he kissed his wife goodbye that morning, told her he'd be home for dinner. Just another day at the office, right?"

Max's chest tightened. He hadn't thought about it like that. Mr. Davis wasn't even supposed to be there. He wasn't part of the plan. He was just another face in the bank, someone standing in the way.

"I'm sure he thought it was just another day," Eli continued, his voice soft but deliberate. "But maybe it wasn't. Maybe that day was supposed to be something more. Maybe he had plans, things he was looking forward to."

Max swallowed, the knot in his throat growing tighter. "Why are you telling me this?"

Eli smiled faintly, but it didn't reach his eyes. "Because sometimes we forget that other people have lives just as complicated, just as messy, as our own."

Max didn't respond. He couldn't. He had spent the last few months telling himself that what he did was necessary, that there had been no other choice. But now, Eli's words were digging into him, unearthing a truth he didn't want to face.

Mr. Davis

Eli's voice took on a different tone, softer, almost nostalgic, as if he were recalling a story from his own past.

"Mr. Davis was a creature of habit, you know. Every morning, he woke up at six sharp, the alarm buzzing beside his bed. He would groan, roll over, and hit the snooze button—just once. That was his routine. He liked those extra ten minutes of sleep, even though he knew he didn't really need them."

Max's brow furrowed, but he didn't interrupt. Something in Eli's voice made him want to listen.

"His wife, Margaret, was already downstairs by the time he got up. She always had coffee ready for him—black, just the way he liked it. They'd sit at the kitchen table together, quietly reading the paper or talking about the little things. How the garden was coming along. How their daughter, Jenna, was doing at college. Simple stuff."

Max's chest felt tight, his heart thudding in his ears. He had never thought of Mr. Davis having a family. The man had always been a nameless figure in his mind, a faceless obstacle. But now, Eli was painting a picture of him—a life, a family, a future.

"Jenna was his pride and joy," Eli continued, his eyes distant, as if he were lost in the story. "He used to talk about her all the time at work. You know, Mr. Davis wasn't always a bank manager. He started off as a teller, working his way up, saving every penny to send Jenna to college. She wanted to be a doctor, just like her uncle. And Mr. Davis? Well, he was more than happy to work those extra hours, take on the extra shifts, just to make sure she had everything she needed."

Max stared out the window, his mind racing. He had never imagined Mr. Davis's life in such detail before. He had been nothing more than someone in the wrong place at the wrong time.

"He worked long hours," Eli said, his voice quieter now. "Sometimes he'd miss dinner, but he always called Margaret to let her know. And when he did make it home, he'd kiss her on the cheek and ask about her day, even if he was too tired to really listen. They had been married for thirty-five years, you know. Thirty-five years, and they still held hands when they walked in the park on Sundays."

Max closed his eyes, trying to shut out Eli's words, but they kept coming, wrapping around him like a vice.

"And then there was this morning," Eli said softly, his voice almost a whisper. "This morning when Mr. Davis kissed Margaret goodbye, just like he always did. He told her he'd be home by six. They had plans, you know. Dinner reservations at that Italian place downtown—the one Margaret loved."

Max's heart pounded in his chest, a sharp pain shooting through him. He could almost see it—the ordinary life Eli was describing, a life that had been ripped apart in an instant.

"He probably wasn't thinking much about work as he headed into the bank," Eli continued, his voice now reflective. "Maybe he was thinking about what he'd order at dinner, or whether he'd have time to pick up that new book Margaret had been talking about. Just another day."

The weight of Eli's words pressed down on Max, suffocating him. He had never allowed himself to think about it this way—about the people who had been affected by his choices. Mr. Davis had always been just a casualty of circumstance, someone unfortunate enough to be caught in the crossfire.

"But did Mr. Davis make it to dinner?" Eli's voice was cold now, cutting through the air like ice. "Unfortunately, this was the day you decided to rob the bank. This was the day his life became part of your plan."

Max's hands shook on the steering wheel, his breath coming in short, shallow bursts. He hadn't thought about Mr. Davis like this. He hadn't wanted to. The man, a casualty of circumstance, someone who just happened to be in the wrong place at the wrong time.

"You never thought about him, did you?" Eli asked quietly, his voice relentless. "You never thought about the fact that Mr. Davis had a family. That he was a husband, a father, a man who had worked his whole life to provide for the people he loved. He wasn't just a bank manager, Max. He was a person. Just like you."

Max's throat tightened, his vision blurring. He had spent months telling himself that the robbery was necessary— that it was the only way to save Eve. But now, with Eli's words echoing in his ears, the guilt was unbearable.

"I didn't want to hurt anyone," Max whispered, his voice barely audible.

Eli nodded slowly, his gaze never leaving Max. "But did you? Whether you meant to or not, you took something from Mr. Davis today. Something he'll never get back."

Max's breath hitched in his throat, the tears welling in his eyes. He had been so focused on his own pain, his own desperation, that he had never stopped to think about the people caught in the crossfire. Mr. Davis had been just another obstacle to the plan. But now, as Eli's words sunk in, he realized that the man behind the counter had been so much more than that.

"You thought you were the only one with something to lose," Eli said quietly, his eyes soft but unrelenting. "But you weren't. Everyone has something to lose, Max. Even people like Mr. Davis."

Max's breath caught in his throat, his chest tight with the weight of it all. He had never thought about it like that before. He had never thought about the lives he had shattered in his desperation to save his own.

"I didn't know," Max whispered, his voice breaking.

Eli nodded. "Maybe not. But now you do."

Eli paused, giving Max a moment to let the weight of his words settle. The silence in the truck became suffocating, pressing in on Max as he fought to contain the emotions threatening to break through. He wanted to push the thoughts away, to focus on the road ahead and not on the devastation he'd caused. But Eli was relentless, peeling back the layers of Max's self-imposed defenses with a quiet but brutal precision.

"What about Jenna?" Eli asked, his voice soft, almost a whisper, but the question landed like a hammer on Max's chest.

Max flinched, a small, involuntary movement that didn't go unnoticed by Eli. He hadn't thought about Mr. Davis's daughter. How could he have? He didn't even know her, didn't know what she looked like, what her laugh sounded like, or how much her father had sacrificed to give her the life she wanted.

"She's supposed to be in her last year of medical school," Eli continued, filling in the gaps Max had refused to consider. "Mr. Davis was so proud. He used to tell his coworkers about her every chance he got—how she'd call him after her anatomy classes, how excited she was to start her residency."

Max's grip on the steering wheel tightened, the leather creaking under the pressure of his fingers. He could feel his heart pounding in his chest, the guilt wrapping around him like a noose. Jenna. Another person he'd never met, another life he had disrupted, another dream he had derailed.

"And now," Eli said, his voice calm but with a quiet intensity, "she'll be getting a call tonight. Not from her father, though. From the police. From someone telling her that her dad won't be coming home. That dinner at that Italian restaurant? That'll never happen."

Max felt the tears welling up in his eyes, blurring the road in front of him. He blinked them away, trying to focus, trying to keep his emotions in check. But it was no use. Eli had cracked something open inside him, something he had been trying to keep buried for too long.

Eli's gaze was steady, compassionate but unyielding. "You've spent so long telling yourself this was the only way. That you had no choice. But you did, Max. You made a choice. And choices have consequences."

Max swallowed hard, his throat dry. He didn't know how to respond. The weight of his actions was crashing down on him like a tidal wave, and he didn't know how to stop it from swallowing him whole.

"You have to live with that now," Eli said, his voice softer, more gentle. "But that doesn't mean it's too late to make a different choice. You can't undo what's been done. But you can decide what you're going to do next."

Max blinked, his vision still blurry from the unshed tears. He didn't know what he was going to do next. He didn't know how to fix the mess he had made. But for the first time, he realized that running wasn't going to solve anything.

Chapter 22: The Breaking Point

The night felt darker now, as if the memories Max was dredging up had thickened the very air around him. The road ahead was barely visible, but he kept driving, his hands gripping the steering wheel tightly. Every mile he drove felt like he was moving deeper into his own mind, unearthing pieces of his past that he had tried to bury. The darkness seemed to stretch beyond the horizon, a vast void that swallowed the headlights of the truck. The hum of the engine was the only thing tethering Max to the present, but even that sound felt distant, like it was coming from a place far outside his body. It was as if the road itself was leading him back, not to any destination on a map, but to the darkest corners of his soul.

Eli remained quiet beside him, his presence steady, unyielding. Max could feel the weight of Eli's silence, the pressure of being examined even when no words were spoken. He could sense Eli's eyes on him, but not in an accusing way—more like Eli was waiting for something to break inside of him. The tension between them felt palpable, as if the truck itself was a fragile vessel carrying the burden of Max's guilt, and at any moment, it might shatter. Max could feel the man's eyes on him, waiting, but there was no pressure. It was as if Eli knew that Max needed to do this in his own time. And yet, the weight of

Eli's words from earlier still lingered—forgive yourself, one promise at a time.

Max swallowed hard. His throat was dry, like the words he needed to say were stuck there, lodged somewhere between his lungs and his heart. Could he really do that? Could he forgive himself for everything that had happened, for all the ways he had failed Eve? The guilt was so familiar now, a constant companion he had carried with him for so long that the thought of living without it felt foreign, almost terrifying. What would he be without it? What would be left of him if he wasn't drowning in this pain? The guilt still gnawed at him, clawing at the edges of his thoughts, refusing to let go.

"I'm not sure if I know how to stop blaming myself," Max muttered, almost to himself. His voice sounded small in the vastness of the night, a confession to the darkness surrounding him. He hadn't meant to say it out loud, but the words slipped through, as if the night itself had coaxed them from him. And now that they were out there, hanging in the air between him and Eli, Max felt exposed in a way that made his skin crawl.

Eli's voice, soft and measured, broke through the stillness. "You won't know until you try."

Max glanced at him, a bitter smile tugging at his lips. There was a hollow edge to that smile, like it was carved from something broken inside of him. "What if I don't deserve to be forgiven?"

Eli's eyes darkened slightly, though his voice remained calm. For a moment, the truck felt smaller, the air thick with the weight of things left unsaid. The silence between them wasn't comforting anymore; it felt like a prelude to something Max didn't want to confront. "That's not for you to decide."

Max opened his mouth to respond, but before he could say anything, a familiar image flashed in his mind—the hospital room. The smell of antiseptic. The cold, sterile light filtering through the window. He could almost hear the faint hum of the fluorescent lights overhead, the smell of cleaning agents mixing with the sour scent of sickness. And Eve, lying there, her skin pale, her eyes dull with exhaustion. The memory slammed into him like a wave, pulling him under, dragging him back to a time when everything had been slipping out of his control. He could feel the chair beneath him, hard and uncomfortable, the plastic of it digging into his legs as he sat there for hours, watching the slow rise and fall of Eve's chest. It was strange how even in the face of death, the mundanity of discomfort could seep in.

***

Max sat at Eve's bedside, his hands gripping hers tightly, as if his very touch could keep her anchored to this world. Her hand felt so small in his, the skin too cold, too fragile. He remembered how her hands used to feel—warm, full of life, the way they would wrap around his when they walked together. Now they felt like paper, as if the slightest pressure would tear her apart. The machines beeped softly in the background, each sound a reminder of how little time they had left. Eve's breathing was shallow, her chest rising and falling with a fragility that terrified him. Every breath she took was labored, each one feeling like it might be her last. It was as if the room itself was holding its breath, waiting for the moment when the machines would fall silent and the inevitable would finally come. The rhythmic beeping seemed to taunt him—every second that passed was a second closer to losing her.

She was so small, so fragile, and Max couldn't bear to look at her like this. She had always been so full of life, her energy infectious, her smile lighting up every room she walked into. Even on her worst days, Eve had been a force of nature, someone who could find joy in the simplest things. But now, that spark was gone. The woman lying in that hospital bed was still Eve, but at the same time, she wasn't. It was like watching a flame burn down to its last ember, flickering weakly before the darkness claimed it. But now, the illness had drained her of everything, leaving her a shadow of the person she used to be. The sight of her like this filled Max with a sense of helplessness that he had never known before.

The doctors had tried everything—treatments, surgeries, medications—but nothing had worked. Nothing could stop the cancer from spreading, from consuming her piece by piece. It had started with hope—whispers of remission, of treatments that might work. But as the months dragged on, hope had become something dangerous, something that only made the fall harder when reality set in. And with each failed attempt, Max's hope had withered, replaced by a hollow, gnawing dread.

And Max… Max had been helpless. He had watched, day after day, as the woman he loved slipped further away from him, and no matter what he did, no matter how hard he tried to fix things, it was never enough. It was like watching her drown, knowing he didn't have the strength to pull her to shore. And yet, he had kept trying, even when the water had closed over her head. He had thought, foolishly, that love would be enough, that his sheer will would somehow keep her alive.

Eve's eyes fluttered open, and she smiled weakly at him, her hand squeezing his gently. The smile was small, barely a shadow of the one he had fallen in love with, but it was still there, still her. It was the same smile that had gotten him through the hardest days, the smile that made him believe in something better. But now, it felt like a final gift, something she was giving him before she let go. "Max," she whispered, her voice barely audible. "You're still here."

Her voice, frail as it was, still held that same warmth, that same gentleness that had always made Max feel like everything would be okay. But now, it didn't comfort him. Now, it felt like a goodbye he wasn't ready to hear.

"Of course I'm here," Max said, his voice trembling with emotion. He could barely get the words out, his throat tight with the weight of everything left unsaid. "I'm not going anywhere."

Eve's smile widened slightly, but there was a sadness in her eyes that Max couldn't ignore. "I know you're trying so hard to save me," she said softly. "But you can't, Max. This isn't something you can fix."

Max shook his head, his heart pounding in his chest. "Don't say that. There's still time. There's still—"

"Max," Eve interrupted, her voice gentle but firm. "It's okay. I'm not afraid."

Max's throat tightened, tears welling in his eyes. "But I am," he admitted, his voice breaking. "I can't lose you, Eve. I don't know how to do this without you."

Eve reached up, her hand resting on his cheek, her touch warm despite her frailness. "You don't have to be afraid. I'm not going anywhere, not really."

Max's heart ached at her words. He knew what she meant. But it didn't feel like enough. It didn't feel like anything would ever be enough.

"I promised I'd take care of you," Max whispered, his voice filled with regret. "I promised I'd protect you."

Eve smiled again, her eyes filled with love. "You have, Max. You've done everything you could. You've always taken care of me."

Max shook his head, his chest tight with the weight of his guilt. "But it wasn't enough."

Eve's hand slipped from his cheek, resting on his chest, just over his heart. "It was more than enough," she whispered. "You've been with me through everything. That's all I ever needed."

Max blinked back tears, his vision blurring. He wanted to believe her, wanted to hold on to her words, but the guilt was too strong. He had failed her. He had promised to protect her, and he had failed.

The beeping of the machines seemed louder now, more insistent, as if they were counting down the minutes, the seconds, until time ran out. The room felt colder, emptier, as if it was already preparing for her absence.

Max closed his eyes, his heart breaking as the reality of the situation crashed over him. He couldn't save her. No matter how hard he tried, no matter how many promises he made, he couldn't stop what was happening. And the helplessness of it all—the futility of his love, his promises—made him feel smaller than he had ever felt.

And he hated himself for it.

The memory faded, and Max was back in the truck, his hands trembling as he gripped the steering wheel. His chest felt tight, his breath coming in short, shallow bursts. The world outside the truck was dark and still, but inside, Max felt like he was drowning in the weight of the past.

Eli remained silent beside him, but Max could feel the weight of the man's presence, steady and unyielding. He wanted to scream, to shout, to tell Eli that none of this was fair. That he had tried so hard to save her, but it had all been for nothing. The world had taken everything from him, and all he had left was the guilt that gnawed at him every day.

But deep down, Max knew that wasn't true. Eve had never asked him to save her. She had never asked him to fix things. All she had wanted was for him to be there with her, to love her, to hold her hand as she faced the inevitable.

And he had been. He had been there, right by her side, through every painful moment. The promises he had made might have been impossible to keep, but that didn't mean he hadn't done his best. And maybe, just maybe, that had been enough.

"She never blamed you," Eli said softly, as if reading Max's thoughts. "You need to stop blaming yourself."

Max shook his head, his vision blurring with tears. "I promised her. I promised I'd protect her, and I couldn't."

Eli's voice was steady, but there was a kindness in it that Max hadn't heard before. "Some promises are impossible to keep. But that doesn't mean you didn't try. And that doesn't mean you failed."

Max swallowed hard, his chest tight with emotion. He had spent so long carrying the weight of his failure, punishing himself for something he had never been able to control. But now, as he sat in the truck, with the memory of Eve's final moments fresh in his mind, he realized something he hadn't been able to accept before.

He had been enough. Maybe he hadn't saved her, maybe he hadn't fixed things the way he had promised, but he had been there. He had loved her. And that had been enough.

"I don't know how to forgive myself," Max admitted, his voice breaking.

Eli's gaze softened. "You start by accepting that you did your best. That you were there when it mattered most."

Max exhaled shakily, the truth of those words sinking in. He didn't know if he could fully forgive himself—not yet—but maybe, just maybe, he could start to let go.

Maybe he could finally stop running.

Chapter 23: Unraveling

The night had grown impossibly dark, the road ahead swallowed by shadows so thick they seemed almost tangible, like black tendrils reaching out to claim the truck. The headlights barely pierced through the gloom, casting feeble beams that were quickly devoured by the desert's vast emptiness. A heavy, oppressive silence had settled inside the truck, broken only by the low rumble of the engine and Max's steady, controlled breathing. He drove on, but it wasn't the road that guided him anymore—it was the memories, each one sharp and jagged, tearing at his insides. They tugged at him, relentless, pulling him deeper into the past. The closer he got to those buried moments, the tighter his chest became, as though the weight of the unresolved emotions was suffocating him from the inside out. Every flashback was like a crack in the dam, the walls he had built to protect himself crumbling under the strain of what he had been avoiding for years.

Eli remained quiet beside him, his presence steady, unyielding, like a shadow cast by a light source that Max could never quite identify. It was as if Eli wasn't really there but was part of the landscape itself—a reflection of Max's own subconscious, pressing him to confront the things he had buried too deep. Even though Max didn't look at him, he could feel Eli's eyes on him, watching, waiting, as if he already knew where Max's mind was going. There was no judgment in his gaze, no impatience, only a quiet, unrelenting persistence that nudged Max closer and closer to the edge of the truth. The air in the truck had grown thick with tension, a palpable energy that hummed between them like static electricity before a storm.

"You're getting closer," Eli said softly, his voice barely cutting through the tension in the truck.

Max frowned, his hands tightening on the steering wheel. "Closer to what?"

"To understanding," Eli replied simply. "To seeing the full picture."

Max's chest tightened. He didn't know if he wanted to see the full picture. Part of him wanted to keep running, to keep burying the past beneath layers of guilt and regret. But he knew, deep down, that there was no escaping this. Not anymore.

"Tell me," Eli said, his voice gentle but firm. "When did you start believing you had to do it all on your own?"

Max blinked, his mind stuttering over the question. He didn't know. Maybe it had always been that way. Or maybe

it had started long before Eve got sick—long before he had
to make impossible choices.

"I don't know," Max muttered. "I just… I thought I had to
fix everything."

Eli nodded, his gaze steady. "Let's go back, then. To when
things first started to slip."

Max didn't want to. He didn't want to relive those
moments—the ones where the weight of responsibility
began to crush him. But before he could protest, the
memories came rushing back, pulling him under.

***

Max stood in the kitchen of their small apartment, staring
blankly at the pile of unpaid bills scattered haphazardly
across the worn, chipped table. The pale light from the
overhead bulb flickered occasionally, casting a sickly,
yellowish glow over the papers that bore nothing but bad
news. The room felt too small, too claustrophobic, as if the
walls themselves were closing in, mirroring the pressure
that had settled over his chest. His heart pounded, the thud
of it echoing in his ears, drowning out everything else.
Each breath felt shallow, forced, as though the air was too
thick to draw in properly. Every unpaid bill, every red

stamp declaring "FINAL NOTICE," was like another stone added to the crushing weight he carried on his shoulders. Rent was overdue. The medical bills were piling up, and each new envelope brought with it a fresh wave of dread. Their savings—what little they had managed to hold on to—was vanishing faster than he could keep track, slipping through his fingers like sand in an hourglass that he couldn't turn back over.

The apartment, once their safe haven, now felt like a cage, its silence oppressive. The faint sounds of the city outside—the occasional honking horn, the distant murmur of voices—felt like reminders of a world that was still moving forward, while Max's had come to a screeching halt. The ticking of the clock on the wall, once comforting, now seemed mocking, each second a reminder that time was running out.

Eve was in the other room, lying on the couch, her frail body barely making an indent in the cushions. The woman who had once danced through life with effortless grace, who had laughed so easily and filled every room she entered with light, was now a shadow of herself. The latest round of treatments had taken everything out of her, leaving her too weak to even stand without help. The vibrant energy that had defined her was gone, replaced by a bone-deep exhaustion that no amount of rest could heal.

Her skin, once glowing with life, was now pale and translucent, stretched thin over her bones. The dark circles under her eyes spoke of sleepless nights, of pain that never seemed to end. Every movement she made was slow, deliberate, as though even the smallest exertion required more strength than she had left to give.

Max couldn't stand to see her like this. He had always admired her strength, her resilience, but now… now, it felt like every day was a losing battle, and no matter how hard she fought, the illness kept taking more and more of her away. The sight of her like this broke something inside him, but he couldn't show it. He had to stay strong, for her sake. He had to keep it together, even as everything around them was falling apart.

Max felt a surge of anger and frustration bubbling up inside him, threatening to boil over. It started as a slow burn in his gut, a twisting knot of helplessness that had been growing for months. He hated this. He hated the feeling of being powerless, of standing on the sidelines while the woman he loved wasted away in front of him. He hated that no matter how many hours he worked, no matter how much he tried to stretch every dollar, it was never enough. There was always another bill, another appointment, another round of treatment that drained both their bank account and their hope. It was as if the universe was conspiring against them, throwing one obstacle after another in their path, and Max couldn't keep up. The pressure was relentless, a constant, suffocating weight pressing down on him from all sides.

He clenched his fists, his nails digging into his palms, the pain sharp and grounding. But even that wasn't enough to quiet the storm inside him. The anger wasn't just at the situation—it was at himself. For not being able to do more. For not being able to fix things. For failing her.

"I'm sorry."

Eve's voice startled him, and he turned to see her standing in the doorway, leaning heavily against the frame. She looked so small, so fragile, and the sight of her like that broke his heart.

Max swallowed hard, his throat tight. "You don't have to be sorry. This isn't your fault."

Eve's eyes filled with tears, and she shook her head. "But it feels like it is. Like I'm dragging you down with me."

Max crossed the room in an instant, pulling her into his arms, holding her as tightly as he dared. "You're not dragging me down, Eve. I'm right here. I'll always be right here."

Eve rested her head against his chest, her body trembling slightly. "I just wish it didn't have to be like this. I wish I could do more."

Max closed his eyes, his heart breaking at her words. He wished he could do more, too. But the truth was, he felt helpless. He had promised to protect her, to take care of her, but nothing he did seemed to make a difference.

"I'll figure it out," Max said quietly, his voice trembling with the weight of the lie. "I'll make this right."

Eve pulled back slightly, looking up at him with sad, knowing eyes. "Max, you don't have to fix everything."

Max's jaw tightened. "Yes, I do. It's my job to take care of you."

Eve shook her head, her eyes filled with love and sorrow. "All I need is you. I don't need you to fix anything. I just need you to be here with me."

But Max couldn't hear her. He couldn't let go of the need to fix things, to make everything right. He had always been the one who had to shoulder the burden, who had to keep everything together. And now, with Eve slipping away, that pressure had become unbearable.

He kissed her forehead, trying to push the fear and guilt to the back of his mind. "I'll make this right," he repeated, even though he knew, deep down, that he couldn't.

The memory faded, and Max was left in the present, his heart aching with the weight of it all. He had tried so hard to be the one who fixed everything, the one who carried all the weight. But in the end, that pressure had only driven him further from Eve, further from what really mattered.

Eli's voice broke the silence. "You couldn't fix it, Max. And you didn't have to."

Max exhaled shakily, his hands trembling on the steering wheel. "But I wanted to. I wanted to save her."

Eli nodded. "Of course you did. But sometimes, saving someone isn't about fixing the problem. Sometimes, it's about being there. Just being present."

Max swallowed hard, his chest tight. "I thought I had to do more."

"You thought you had to do it alone," Eli corrected, his voice steady. "But you didn't. She never asked that of you."

Max's vision blurred with unshed tears. He had spent so long carrying the burden of his promises, of the need to fix everything. But maybe, just maybe, Eve had never needed him to do that. Maybe all she had needed was him.

"I failed her," Max whispered, his voice barely audible. "I wasn't enough."

Eli's gaze softened, and he reached out, placing a hand on Max's shoulder. "You were more than enough. You just couldn't see it then."

Max closed his eyes, a tear slipping down his cheek. He wanted to believe Eli. He wanted to believe that he had been enough for Eve, that his presence had meant something, even if he couldn't fix everything. But the guilt still weighed heavy on his heart, and he didn't know if he could ever truly let it go.

"Maybe it's time to forgive yourself," Eli said gently. "Maybe it's time to let go."

Max didn't respond. He didn't know if he could. But the truth was there, just beneath the surface, waiting for him to acknowledge it.

And maybe, just maybe, he was ready to try.

Chapter 24: The Things We Couldn't Fix

The night had grown impossibly dark, the road ahead swallowed by shadows. Max drove in silence, his mind a whirlwind of memories, each one pulling him deeper into the past. The truck's headlights cut through the blackness like fragile beams, the world beyond barely visible. The hum of the engine was a constant, but it did nothing to drown out the noise inside Max's head. Every thought, every moment Eli had been guiding him toward, collided into a storm of emotions that threatened to break him.

He gripped the steering wheel harder, the tension in his hands mirroring the tightness in his chest. He could feel Eli's steady presence beside him, the quiet persistence of his unspoken challenge. Max had long grown accustomed to running, to pushing everything down, but Eli was pulling him back—back toward the truths Max had spent years burying.

Max's jaw clenched as his knuckles turned white against the worn leather of the wheel. Every mile he drove felt like he was moving deeper into his own mind, like the truck was carrying him not through physical space, but through the darkest corridors of his soul. The road was becoming a metaphor for the path he had avoided for so long—one filled with pain, regret, and the memories he didn't want to face.

Eli had been quiet for a long time, but the weight of his presence remained palpable, like the feeling of a storm about to break. Max knew that when Eli spoke again, it would cut right to the heart of the matter, as it always did.

Finally, Eli broke the silence, his voice low but steady, cutting through the tension in the cab. "You're getting closer," he said, his words like a calm wave lapping at the shore, inviting Max to wade deeper into the truth.

Max frowned, unsure of what Eli meant but knowing that it wasn't something simple. "Closer to what?" he asked, his voice rough, as if dredging up words was as difficult as facing his memories.

Eli didn't turn to look at him. Instead, he kept his gaze forward, fixed on the dark road ahead. "To understanding," Eli replied simply. "To seeing the full picture."

Max's heart clenched in his chest. The full picture? He wasn't sure he wanted to see that. The pieces he had glimpsed so far—the weight of Eve's illness, the guilt of his failures—were more than enough to crush him. What would happen if he finally saw everything, if he allowed himself to truly face the entirety of what he had been avoiding?

"I don't know if I want to see it," Max admitted, his voice barely above a whisper, as if speaking the words aloud might summon the full force of the truth.

Eli's voice remained calm, almost soothing. "You need to see it," he said. "Only then will you understand why you've been running."

Max's chest tightened. Running. That's what he had been doing for years—running from the memories, from the loss, from the realization that no matter how hard he tried, he couldn't fix everything. He had built his life around that need for control, for saving what he could. But now, the foundations of those beliefs were crumbling.

Eli let the silence stretch for a moment before asking the question Max had been dreading. "Tell me, when did you start believing you had to do it all on your own?"

Max's breath caught in his throat, his heart pounding in his ears. The answer wasn't something he could easily articulate. When had it started? Maybe it had always been that way. Or maybe it had begun long before Eve's illness —back when he was just a boy.

His mind drifted, unbidden, back to his childhood. Back to the moment that had shaped him more than any other. The moment when helplessness first became a constant in his life.

***

Max was ten years old, sitting by his mother's bedside in their small, sunlit home. The curtains fluttered softly in the summer breeze, and the light that filtered through them bathed the room in a warm glow. It was the kind of day that might have seemed beautiful, serene, if not for the overwhelming sadness that lingered in the air.

The room smelled faintly of the roses his father grew in the garden—his mother's favorite. But even the sweet scent of the flowers couldn't mask the smell of sickness, of the hospital-grade antiseptic that seemed to cling to everything now. The bed, the air, his mother's pale skin.

She lay still, her breaths shallow, but when she turned her head to look at Max, she smiled. Her hand trembled slightly as she reached out to him, but her eyes were as warm as ever.

"Come here, Max," she whispered, her voice no longer the strong, confident sound it had been just a few months ago. Now it was soft, fragile, like the light touch of a butterfly's wing.

Max climbed onto the bed beside her, curling up against her side. Even though her body felt smaller, frailer than it ever had before, her arms still felt safe, like nothing could hurt him as long as she was holding him.

But Max knew better. He had heard the whispers, the conversations between his father and the doctors when they thought he wasn't listening. His mother was sick—very sick—and no one had said it outright, but Max had started to understand that there were some things that even adults couldn't fix.

His mother stroked his hair gently, humming a lullaby that Max had heard countless times before, but now it sounded different. It wasn't just a song. It was a goodbye.

"Are you going to be okay, Mom?" Max asked, his voice small and uncertain.

His mother smiled again, though it didn't quite reach her eyes this time. "Of course, honey," she said softly. "I'll always be with you."

Max frowned, not understanding. How could she always be with him if she wasn't going to be there? He didn't know how to ask the question that was lodged in his chest, the fear that was starting to grow inside him like a vine wrapping around his heart.

But his mother didn't explain. She just held him a little tighter, and Max closed his eyes, trying to believe her words even though they didn't make sense.

***

The room felt impossibly small, as if the walls themselves were closing in around Max, shrinking with each shallow breath his mother took. The summer light that streamed in through the curtains, once so warm and golden, now seemed harsh, too bright, almost intrusive in its beauty. Outside, the world carried on—birds chirped in the garden, a soft breeze rustled the leaves of the old oak tree—but inside, time had slowed, thickened, as if the very air had become syrupy and heavy, clinging to everything, making it hard to move, hard to breathe.

Max sat by her bedside, his small hand clasped in hers, his fingers dwarfed by her once-strong grip, now weak and trembling. He could feel the coolness of her skin, the faint tremor that ran through her body, and it filled him with a fear he had never known. Her breaths were faint, each one a struggle, as though her lungs were fighting against the weight of the world. The sound of it, that soft rasp, echoed in the silence of the room like a ticking clock—each breath counting down to something Max didn't want to understand.

Outside the window, the roses his father had planted swayed gently in the breeze, their deep red petals stark against the fading light of the evening. They were her favorite—the ones she used to gather in bundles, filling the house with their fragrance. But now, the scent of those roses felt oppressive, mingling with the sharp, antiseptic smell of sickness that had invaded the room, smothering any trace of the life that once filled this space.

Max's eyes flicked toward the door, half-expecting his father to come rushing in, to say something, to do something, but there was only silence. The house, so full of life and noise just months ago, now felt hollow, like a shell that had been emptied of everything that mattered.

His mother shifted slightly, her hand squeezing his just a little tighter, and Max's heart leapt into his throat. Her eyes fluttered open, the deep brown that once held warmth and laughter now dull, clouded by the weight of too many sleepless nights. But even in the midst of it all, she smiled. It was small, weak, but it was there, and for a moment, Max almost believed that everything would be okay.

But then he saw the truth. It was in her eyes—an exhaustion so deep it seemed to reach into her very soul. She wasn't just tired. She was leaving, slipping away with each breath, and Max could feel it, could sense the life draining out of her like water seeping through his fingers. He wanted to say something, to scream, to beg her not to go, but the words caught in his throat, trapped by the lump that had been growing there for days.

The sunlight outside began to fade, casting long shadows across the room, stretching toward them like dark fingers reaching through the cracks in the window. The breeze that had once been gentle now felt sharp, cold, biting at the edges of the room, and Max shivered despite the warmth of the day.

And then, in the quiet stillness of the moment, Max felt her grip loosen.

His heart pounded in his chest, a frantic rhythm that seemed too loud, too fast in the otherwise silent room. He looked up at her, panic surging through him as her eyes fluttered shut, her breathing becoming shallow, uneven. He leaned closer, his small body pressing against hers, as if somehow his presence could pull her back from the edge, could keep her here with him just a little longer.

But the truth was inescapable.

Her chest rose one final time, a slow, painful inhale, and then… stillness.

The room seemed to hold its breath, the air thick with the weight of the moment. Max stared at her, his mind refusing to accept what he knew had just happened. Her hand still rested in his, but it was different now—heavier, cooler. The life that had once filled her, the energy and warmth that had been his world, was gone, and in its place was an emptiness that seemed to swallow everything.

The world outside continued on. The birds still sang. The roses still swayed in the breeze. But inside, everything had changed. Max sat frozen, unable to move, unable to breathe, his eyes fixed on her still form, waiting for something—anything—that would bring her back.

But there was nothing. Only silence. Only stillness.

The last light of the sun slipped below the horizon, plunging the room into a deep, suffocating darkness. And in that darkness, Max sat alone, the weight of everything pressing down on him, heavier than anything he had ever known.

The memory faded, but the weight of it remained, settling heavily in Max's chest. That had been the first time he had truly felt helpless, the first time he had realized that no matter how much he loved someone, no matter how much he wanted to protect them, there were some things he couldn't control.

And when Eve got sick, it was like all of those old fears came rushing back, stronger than ever. The fear of losing someone he loved. The fear of not being enough. The fear that no matter how hard he tried, he would fail.

Eli's voice was soft, pulling Max back to the present. "You couldn't save your mother," he said quietly. "And you couldn't save Eve. That's why you've been running."

Max clenched his teeth, his hands gripping the steering wheel so tightly that his hands were numb. "I thought if I just tried hard enough, I could stop it," he admitted, his voice strained.

"But some things aren't meant to be stopped," Eli replied, his tone gentle but firm. "Some things have to be accepted."

Max swallowed hard, the truth of Eli's words cutting deep. He had spent so long trying to fight, to fix, to control everything around him. But there were some battles he couldn't win, some losses he couldn't prevent. And that realization hurt more than anything.

But there was another memory—a deeper wound that still ached. The loss that Max had never fully processed, the one that had torn at the seams of his and Eve's dreams.

***

Max stood in the hallway outside the doctor's office, the sterile smell of antiseptic filling his nostrils. His hands trembled as he stared at the test results in his hands, his mind refusing to accept the words printed on the page.

Beside him, Eve sat in silence, her face pale and tear-streaked. Her eyes were red from crying, and she clutched a tissue in her hands as if it were the only thing keeping her from falling apart completely. Max had never seen her look so defeated.

The results were clear. They wouldn't be able to have children. Months of trying, of hoping, of dreaming of the family they would build together, had all led to this—the crushing realization that those dreams would never come true.

Max's heart felt like it was being ripped out of his chest. He had promised Eve the world. He had promised her a future, a family. But now, as he stood in the hallway of that cold, impersonal clinic, all of those promises felt hollow. He had failed her. Again.

"I'm sorry," he whispered, his voice thick with emotion. He couldn't bring himself to look at her. He couldn't face the pain in her eyes.

Eve reached for his hand, squeezing it tightly. "It's not your fault," she said softly, her voice hoarse. "We'll find another way. We'll be okay."

But Max couldn't shake the feeling that it was his fault. That he had failed her, just like he had failed his mother. The guilt gnawed at him, consuming him from the inside out.

Back in the present, Max's heart pounded, his chest felt like it was being crushed under the weight of all the things he had tried so hard to control. The memories felt like chains, wrapping around him, pulling him down into the depths of his regret. He had spent so much of his life trying to fix things, trying to control the uncontrollable. But in the end, all he had done was run from the truth.

Eli's voice was calm, but there was a warmth in it now, a gentleness that Max hadn't noticed before. "You thought you had to do it alone," Eli said. "But you didn't. She never asked you to."

Max closed his eyes, a tear slipping down his cheek. He had spent so long carrying the burden of his promises, the weight of his failures. But maybe—just maybe—he hadn't failed at all.

Chapter 25: Dreams Deferred

The road stretched endlessly before them, a narrow line of pavement swallowed by the night. The headlights of the truck pierced through the thick darkness, casting weak beams that barely touched the black void ahead. It was as if the world beyond the reach of those lights didn't exist, as if the road beneath the truck's tires was leading them into some uncharted abyss. Max could feel the weight of everything pressing down on him.

The quiet hum of the engine filled the space between him and Eli, the rhythmic vibrations of the road under the tires offering a temporary distraction from the turmoil brewing inside him. But the silence between them wasn't oppressive—it was expectant, pregnant with the weight of the unspoken truths that Eli seemed to be patiently waiting for Max to confront. There was no urgency in Eli's demeanor, but Max could feel the quiet pressure building. Eli wasn't going to let him escape what was coming.

Max's thoughts churned, a whirlwind of fractured memories, images, and emotions he had been trying to outrun for so long. He had spent so much of his life running—away from the guilt, away from the pain of his failures. But now, here in this truck, with the darkness closing in on all sides, it felt like he was running out of road. There was nowhere left to go.

"You always wanted to fix things," Eli said quietly, his voice slipping into the quiet like a knife slicing through the fog of Max's mind. It wasn't a question, just a simple statement. And it cut deep.

Max's jaw clenched. The weight of those words landed heavily, like a rock sinking to the bottom of his chest. He didn't need Eli to explain. He knew exactly what he meant. He had spent his entire life trying to fix things—trying to be the one in control, the one who could protect the people he loved from the chaos of the world. But some things, Max was learning, couldn't be fixed.

Eli turned his head slightly, his gaze resting on Max, unblinking but not unkind. "But there was one thing you couldn't fix, wasn't there?"

Max didn't answer at first. He stared at the road ahead, the narrow strip of asphalt that seemed to stretch into infinity, but his mind wasn't on the road. His mind was on the past —on the one thing that had unraveled everything, the one thing he had promised but couldn't deliver.

His hands tightened on the wheel, his breath hitching slightly as memories began to surface again. The fertility treatments, the doctor's visits, the endless cycles of hope and disappointment. Each moment, each failure, was like a dagger lodged deeper into his chest. He had wanted so desperately to give Eve a family. He had promised her a future filled with laughter, with the sound of tiny feet running through their home, but that dream had slipped through his fingers, no matter how tightly he had tried to hold on to it.

Max swallowed hard, the familiar ache in his chest deepening. He had never stopped wanting to fix things. Even when it became clear that some things were out of his control, he had kept fighting. He had fought because he didn't know how to stop. He didn't know how to let go.

"You never really stopped, did you?" Eli's voice was soft, but there was a quiet understanding in it. "Even when it was beyond your control."

Max blinked, his throat tight, the memories swirling around him like a storm he couldn't escape. He hadn't stopped trying, not even after the doctor had told them the truth.

***

Max sat beside Eve in the cold, sterile room, his hands gripping hers tightly as if his touch alone could keep her anchored to hope. The clock on the wall ticked relentlessly, its sound echoing in the quiet room like a heartbeat, each second passing feeling like a small eternity. Max had lost count of how many times they had been here, how many times they had held their breath, waiting for news, for some sliver of hope.

But now, as the doctor entered the room, her face kind but serious, Max felt the familiar twist of dread in his stomach. He braced himself, knowing—deep down—that this time, hope wasn't coming.

The doctor sat down across from them, her eyes filled with the kind of sympathy that only made things worse. She folded her hands in front of her, her voice gentle but firm, as if she had said these words too many times before. "I'm sorry," she began, her voice low, but the impact of those words hit Max like a tidal wave. "The results are conclusive. We've explored every option, and at this point, it's unlikely that you'll be able to conceive naturally."

Max felt the air leave his lungs as if someone had punched him in the gut. His vision blurred slightly, the doctor's words fading into the background. He could hear her talking—explaining alternatives, offering other options—but it all sounded distant, like it was coming from underwater. He could barely register anything beyond the crushing weight of what they had just lost.

He glanced at Eve. She was staring down at her hands, her fingers intertwined in her lap, her face pale and tight with unshed tears. Max's heart broke for her. He knew how much she had wanted this—how much they had both wanted this. A family. A future. It was the one thing they had both dreamed of for so long, and now it was gone.

After the appointment, they walked out of the clinic in silence, the weight of the news pressing down on them like a suffocating blanket. Max didn't know what to say. He didn't know how to comfort her when he felt so utterly lost himself. The future they had imagined, the life they had been building together, was slipping away, and he had no idea how to stop it.

The memory hit Max like a tidal wave, pulling him under and dragging him back into the present, where the ache in his chest was as real as it had been in that doctor's office. He blinked, his hands gripping the steering wheel even tighter as if holding on to it would somehow keep him grounded in this moment, rather than the memories that were threatening to consume him.

"I thought if I just tried hard enough," Max whispered, his voice thick with emotion, "I could still give her the life we wanted."

Eli didn't respond right away. He let the silence stretch between them, a gentle reminder that there was no rush. Max could feel Eli's eyes on him, steady and patient, like a quiet presence that refused to let him drown in his own guilt.

"But the harder you tried," Eli finally said, his voice calm but pointed, "the more distant it became."

Max swallowed hard, the truth of those words sinking into him like cold water. He had been so focused on fixing everything—on making things right—that he hadn't seen how much he was losing in the process. The more he tried to control the future, the more the present slipped away.

"I thought I had to make it right," Max whispered, his voice trembling. "I thought if I could fix it, she'd be happy."

Eli turned toward him, his gaze unwavering. "And when you couldn't, you felt like you failed."

Max's chest tightened, his breath coming in shallow gasps. "I did fail. I promised her a family, a future. I promised I'd protect her, and I couldn't give her any of that."

The silence that followed was thick with the weight of Max's confession. He had never said those words out loud before, not even to himself. But now, here in the dark with Eli beside him, the truth hung in the air, undeniable and suffocating.

Eli's voice was gentle, but it carried a weight that made Max's heart ache. "You didn't fail her, Max. She didn't want the family you couldn't give her. She wanted you."

Max blinked, the tears he had been holding back for so long finally slipping free, blurring his vision. He had been so focused on the life they couldn't have—the child they would never hold—that he had lost sight of what had really mattered. Eve had never asked him for perfection. She had never asked him to fix everything. All she had wanted was for him to be there with her. To love her. To hold her through the pain, through the disappointment. But Max, in his desperation to fix things, had been too blind to see it.

***

Max stood in the doorway of the empty room, his heart heavy as he stared at the bare walls, the untouched space that was supposed to have been the nursery. The room was silent, the kind of silence that felt thick and oppressive, like it was pressing down on him from all sides. The crib they had picked out remained un-purchased, the walls still the neutral color they had painted, undecorated and lifeless.

Max hadn't come into this room for months. He had avoided it, afraid of what it represented. But now, standing here, the weight of it all felt unbearable. The dream they had shared, the life they had imagined for themselves—it was gone. And Max didn't know how to face it.

Eve appeared behind him, her footsteps soft but sure. She came up beside him, resting a hand on his arm. Her touch was warm, but it couldn't chase away the cold feeling of failure that gripped Max's heart.

"I'm sorry," Max whispered, his voice trembling. "I promised you a family. I promised we'd have this…"

Eve turned him to face her, her eyes filled with a love that made his heart ache even more. "You don't have to apologize," she said softly. "This doesn't change anything."

Max shook his head, tears slipping down his cheeks as the guilt he had been carrying finally broke free. "But I wanted to give you everything. I wanted to fix this."

Eve cupped his face in her hands, her voice steady and full of understanding. "We don't need this to be happy, Max. We don't need a baby to be a family. We have each other. That's enough."

Max's breath hitched, his heart shattering under the weight of her words. He had been so focused on what they had lost that he hadn't seen what they still had. He hadn't been able to give her the future they had dreamed of, but he had given her his love, his presence. And maybe that had been enough all along.

The memory faded, and Max was back in the truck, the weight of everything settling over him like a heavy blanket. His heart ached, his chest tight with the grief and guilt he had carried for so long. But for the first time, there was a sliver of light breaking through the darkness.

"You were enough, Max," Eli said softly, his voice filled with quiet understanding. "You didn't need to give her a child or fix the world. You gave her you."

Max swallowed hard, his vision blurring with tears. He had spent so long believing he had failed, so long carrying the weight of promises he couldn't keep. But now, for the first time, he could see it—Eve hadn't needed him to fix anything. She had only needed him. His love. His presence.

"I didn't see it then," Max whispered, his voice thick with emotion. "I thought I had to fix everything."

Eli's gaze softened, his eyes full of compassion. "But you see it now."

Max nodded slowly, the truth settling into his bones like a long-overdue acceptance. He had spent years trying to run from his failures, from the promises he couldn't keep. But now, he could see a path forward. It wasn't about fixing everything. It was about being there, about loving the people he cared about, even when he couldn't control the outcome.

"I don't know if I can forgive myself," Max admitted, his voice barely audible.

Eli leaned back in his seat, his gaze never leaving Max's. "You're closer than you think."

Chapter 26: The Edge of Control

The road stretched endlessly before them, a ribbon of black stretching out beneath the stars, winding into the vastness of the night. The truck's headlights were barely more than whispers in the dark, their beams cutting through the thick, suffocating black that seemed to swallow everything outside. Beyond the road, the desert was a void, silent and still, an expanse that stretched into nothingness. Max could feel the isolation pressing in on him, the weight of the world closing around him, yet it was nothing compared to the storm raging inside his own mind.

His hands rested on the steering wheel, gripping it tightly, but his focus wasn't on the road. It hadn't been for miles. Instead, his mind churned with the memories Eli had drawn out of him—the moments he had tried so hard to bury, the failures he had never been able to reconcile. The weight of them was like a lead blanket, pulling him down, threatening to suffocate him. He could feel each memory unraveling, pulling apart the carefully constructed walls he had built around himself over the years, walls that had kept him from confronting the truth.

Beside him, Eli sat still and watchful. His presence was steady, unshakable, but not in an oppressive way. It was as if Eli knew there was more Max needed to face—more that he had yet to uncover about himself, about his past. And Eli was simply there, waiting for Max to take the next step. The silence between them was thick, charged with an unspoken understanding. Max could sense that Eli wasn't going to push him, but he wasn't going to let him off the hook, either.

Max let out a long, slow breath, the air leaving his lungs with a heaviness that felt like it had been there for years. His thoughts drifted, pulled in different directions by the fragments of his past that had begun surfacing. He thought of Eve—always Eve—and the love they had shared, the life they had tried to build together. The memories of their early days, full of hope and possibility, seemed like distant dreams now, overshadowed by the losses they had endured, the struggles that had torn them apart piece by piece.

Max clenched his jaw, his chest tightening with the familiar ache of guilt and regret. The child they had never had, the family that had slipped through their fingers—it was all too much. He had tried so hard to hold onto the idea that he could fix it all, that if he just worked harder, if he just did more, he could give Eve the life they had dreamed of. But the harder he tried, the more it seemed to slip away.

"You always wanted to fix things," Eli's voice finally broke through the silence, soft but cutting to the core of Max's thoughts. There was no judgment in his words, just a quiet, undeniable truth that cut deeper than Max expected.

Max glanced at him, his chest tight. The weight of Eli's statement was too heavy to ignore. "Yeah," he muttered, his voice rough, raw. "I did."

Eli's eyes held Max's gaze, calm and unwavering. "But there's nothing left to fix, is there?"

The question hung in the air between them like a thick fog. Max's hands tightened on the wheel, his hands turning pale against the worn leather. It felt like he had been running forever—running from the memories, from the guilt, from the crushing reality that there was nothing more he could do.

"No," Max admitted, his voice barely more than a whisper. "There's nothing left to fix."

Eli nodded slowly, his expression unreadable. "So why are you still trying?"

Max didn't have an answer. He didn't know why. He had spent so long trying to hold everything together, trying to control every aspect of his life, that it had become instinctual. But now, as the memories resurfaced, he could see how futile it all had been. How it had pushed him further from the things that really mattered. How it had blinded him to the truth.

"There's one more thing," Eli said, his voice almost a whisper now, but it was weighted with something inevitable, something Max knew he couldn't avoid any longer. "One more moment you haven't faced."

Max's stomach twisted. His heart pounded in his chest, the rhythm erratic as anxiety crept in. He knew exactly what Eli meant. There was one more memory. One more piece of the past that he had locked away, too painful, too raw to confront. It was the moment that had driven him to the edge, the moment when everything had fallen apart.

The night of the fight.

The air in the truck felt heavier as the memory began to rise to the surface, unbidden but unstoppable. Max could almost feel the oppressive tension from that night, as if it were still wrapped around him like a vice, squeezing tighter with every breath.

***

Max sat in the dimly lit living room of their apartment, the soft glow of a single lamp casting long shadows across the room. Outside, the faint sound of rain tapped against the window, the rhythm steady but distant, almost as if it were trying to lull him into a false sense of calm. But there was no calm to be found here. The tension between him and Eve had been building for days—weeks, maybe. And now, it felt like a storm waiting to break.

Max leaned forward, his head in his hands, elbows resting on his knees. His heart pounded in his chest, each beat a painful reminder of how much was slipping through his fingers. He had promised Eve so much. He had promised her a future, a family. He had promised to take care of her, to protect her. And now, it felt like everything was falling apart, crumbling into dust.

The door to the bedroom creaked open, and Max looked up to see Eve standing in the doorway. Her face was pale, drawn, the weariness of their struggles etched into every line. She looked at him, her eyes filled with sadness—and something else. Something Max didn't want to face.

Eve stepped into the living room, her footsteps soft against the floor, but her presence filled the space like a force that Max couldn't escape. "We can't keep doing this," she said softly, her voice trembling slightly, but there was a strength behind her words that made Max's chest tighten.

Max lifted his head, his throat dry. "What do you mean?" The question felt like a lifeline, something to cling to, even though he knew exactly what she meant.

Eve took a deep breath, her eyes never leaving his. "You're trying so hard to fix everything, Max. But you're not here. You're not with me."

The words hit him like a punch to the gut, knocking the wind out of him. He blinked, confusion and frustration swirling in his chest. "What are you talking about? I'm doing everything I can for us. I'm trying to—"

"You're trying to control everything," Eve interrupted, her voice growing firmer, though the tears in her eyes betrayed the emotion she was holding back. "You're trying to control something you can't fix. And it's tearing us apart."

Max stood abruptly, his hands shaking as he ran them through his hair. "I'm doing this for you, Eve. For us. I can't just sit back and do nothing while everything falls apart!"

Eve's tears slipped down her cheeks, her voice breaking as she spoke. "But that's all I need, Max. I need you to stop trying to fix things. I need you to be here with me, to just be present. That's all I've ever needed."

Max's heart ached at her words, but he couldn't let go of the need to fix it all. He couldn't bear the thought of losing her, of watching her slip away like his mother had. He had to do something. He had to be the one to make it right.

"I can't lose you," Max whispered, his voice trembling. "I can't just watch it all fall apart."

Eve stepped closer, her hand resting on his cheek. Her touch was warm, grounding, even as her own emotions threatened to overwhelm her. "You won't lose me, Max," she said softly. "I'm right here. But I need you to be with me. Not with your plans, not with your need to control everything. I need you."

Max's breath hitched, tears stinging his eyes. He had wanted so badly to protect her, to save her from the pain, from the illness that was consuming her. But in his desperation, he had lost sight of what really mattered.

"I'm scared," Max admitted, his voice barely audible. "I'm scared of losing you."

Eve's hand gently stroked his cheek, her eyes filled with love. "I know. But you're not going to lose me. I'll always be with you, Max. No matter what happens."

Max closed his eyes, a tear slipping down his cheek. He had been so focused on the fear, on the need to control everything, that he hadn't seen what was right in front of him. Eve's love. Her presence. The moments they still had together.

"I'm sorry," Max whispered, his voice breaking. "I'm so sorry."

Eve smiled through her tears, her hand resting over his heart. "I forgive you, Max. But you have to forgive yourself."

Back in the present, Max's chest felt tight, his breath coming in short, shallow bursts. That night had been the turning point. It was when he had realized, too late, that all Eve had ever wanted was for him to be with her—not to fix things, not to control the world around them, but to be present, to love her.

And he had been so afraid of losing her that he had almost missed it.

"You were so focused on the fear," Eli said softly. "But fear doesn't control love, Max. You don't have to keep running from it."

Max swallowed hard, his throat tight with emotion. "I was afraid I wasn't enough."

Eli's gaze softened. "But you were. You were enough for Eve. You always were."

Max exhaled slowly, his hands trembling as he loosened his grip on the wheel. He had been running for so long— running from his fear, from his guilt, from the belief that he had failed. But the truth was there, right in front of him.

He had been enough. He had loved Eve, and that had been enough.

"I don't know how to let go of the fear," Max whispered, his voice thick with emotion.

Eli leaned back, his eyes never leaving Max's. "You don't have to let go all at once. You just have to stop holding on so tightly."

Max closed his eyes, a tear slipping down his cheek. For the first time, he could feel the weight lifting. He wasn't ready to let go completely. But he could feel the possibility. He could feel the space where forgiveness might live, where peace might finally find him.

And maybe, just maybe, he was ready to take the first step.

Chapter 27: A Whisper of What Could Have Been

The night pressed on, the dark expanse of the road stretching endlessly in front of them. The headlights of the truck barely cut through the inky blackness, as if the world outside had been swallowed whole by the void. The stars above seemed distant, their light too faint to touch the earth. Max now resting his hands some on the steering wheel , the leather cool against his palms, grounding him in the present, even as his mind wandered far away, into the recesses of his past.

The world outside the truck felt distant, almost unreal, as if the only things that existed were the memories swirling in Max's mind and the quiet presence of Eli beside him. The silence between them wasn't oppressive—it was thick with unspoken questions and unresolved pain. The hum of the engine was the only sound, a steady rhythm that matched the pounding in Max's chest. The road stretched on, an endless ribbon, but Max felt as if he were driving in circles, moving forward yet going nowhere at all.

Max's thoughts were tangled—threads of the past weaving together with the present, creating a knot in his chest that tightened with every mile. He had spent so long trying to outrun his guilt, trying to control the uncontrollable, that now, sitting in this truck with Eli, he felt like he was standing on the edge of something profound. The fear, the pain, the loss—all of it was catching up to him, looming like shadows just beyond the reach of the headlights.

The memories felt like weights pulling him down, threatening to drown him. Max's mind flickered back to moments long buried—the arguments with Eve, the crushing disappointment of the child that would never be, and the slow, painful unraveling of the life they had once dreamed of together.

Eli had been silent for a while, but Max could feel his presence—a calm, steady force beside him, unwavering in the storm of Max's emotions. There was something about Eli that felt both familiar and foreign at the same time. It was as though Eli knew things—things about Max's life, about Eve—that no one else could possibly know. The thought gnawed at Max, and with every mile they traveled, the feeling only grew stronger.

Max's knuckles tightened on the steering wheel yet again. He couldn't ignore it anymore. He had to ask.

"How do you know so much about me?" Max asked suddenly, his voice breaking the silence. The question had been gnawing at him for a while now, and he couldn't shake the feeling that there was more to Eli than he had first realized. His voice felt small in the vastness of the night, the weight of the question hanging between them like a stone.

Eli didn't answer right away. He simply stared out at the road ahead, his face unreadable. Max stole a glance at him, noticing the way the faint glow of the dashboard lights cast soft shadows across Eli's features, giving him an otherworldly quality that sent a shiver down Max's spine.

"I've been with you for a long time," Eli said quietly, almost as if the words weren't meant to be fully heard. His tone was calm, but there was something beneath it—something unsettling, like the feeling of being watched when you're alone.

Max frowned, confusion flickering through him. "What do you mean? I've never seen you before." He shifted in his seat, unease creeping into his gut. How could this man, this stranger, claim to have been with him for so long? It didn't make sense.

Eli's lips curled into the faintest of smiles, but there was something distant in his eyes, a sadness that Max hadn't noticed before. "Not in the way you think."

Max's heart skipped a beat. There was something unsettling about Eli's words, something that made the hair on the back of his neck stand up. He opened his mouth to ask another question, but before he could, another memory began to surface, pulling him under. It came unbidden, like a wave crashing over him, sweeping him back to a time he had tried so hard to forget.

***

Max sat in their small living room, the light of a dim lamp casting long shadows across the walls. The soft ticking of the clock on the mantle echoed through the room, each second stretching longer than the last. Outside, the world moved on, indifferent to the silent storm brewing inside their home. It had been another long day—one of many spent in silence. Eve sat across from him, her body curled up on the couch, her legs tucked beneath her as she stared out the window, lost in her own thoughts. Her fingers absentmindedly traced the rim of the coffee cup in her hands, though she hadn't taken a sip in hours.

They hadn't spoken much lately. The weight of everything —her illness, the loss of their chance at a family, the fear of what was coming—had settled between them like a heavy fog. It was the kind of silence that suffocated, that pressed in from all sides until there was no room left to breathe.

Max wanted to say something, anything, to bridge the gap that had formed between them. He could feel it widening with every passing day, the distance between them growing even though they were sitting just feet apart. But every time he opened his mouth, the words felt hollow. What could he say that would make things better? What could he possibly do to fix this?

"I miss the way things used to be," Eve said suddenly, her voice soft but filled with sadness. The sound of her voice broke through the heavy silence, startling Max out of his thoughts.

Max looked at her, his chest tightening. "I do too," he admitted, his voice barely more than a whisper. The truth of it weighed heavy on him. They had both been clinging to the past, to the life they had imagined, the life that now seemed like a distant dream.

Eve's gaze drifted to the empty space in the room—the corner where they had once imagined a crib, where they had talked about what their life would look like with a child. The plans they had made, the names they had picked out—it was all still there, lingering like ghosts in the air. But that future was gone now, lost in the shuffle of doctor visits and missed opportunities.

"We could have had a beautiful life," Eve whispered, her voice thick with emotion. Her eyes shimmered with unshed tears, but she blinked them away, refusing to let them fall.

Max swallowed hard, his throat tight. He glanced at the empty corner, the space that had once held so much promise, and felt the familiar pang of loss settle deep in his chest. "We still can," he said, but even as the words left his mouth, he didn't believe them. The hope they had once shared had been replaced by a hollow ache that he couldn't shake, no matter how hard he tried.

Eve didn't respond. She simply stared at that empty space, as if she could see the child they never had—the one they had dreamed of, the one that had slipped away.

The memory faded, but the ache in Max's chest remained, a dull, persistent throb that he had carried with him for years. That moment, that quiet, unspoken pain, had haunted him for so long. He had promised Eve so much, and now, all that was left were the empty spaces where their dreams should have been.

Eli's Insight

"You think about that a lot, don't you?" Eli's voice cut through the silence, his tone gentle but probing, as if he had seen the very memory Max had just relived.

Max blinked, his heart pounding. How could Eli know? How could he possibly understand the depth of that pain? "What do you mean?"

"The life you could have had. The family. The child."

Max's breath caught in his throat. Eli's words hit too close to home, stirring emotions he had tried so hard to bury. He glanced at Eli, confusion and unease swirling inside him. "How do you know about that?"

Eli didn't look at him. His gaze remained fixed on the road ahead, but there was a quiet sadness in his voice when he spoke again. "I know more than you think, Max."

Max's chest tightened, his mind racing. There was something about the way Eli spoke—something that felt familiar in a way that Max couldn't explain. He had spent so long running from the pain, from the loss of the life they had imagined, but now, sitting here with Eli, it felt like all those buried emotions were rising to the surface.

"Who are you?" Max asked, his voice trembling slightly.

Eli didn't answer right away. He simply turned his head, his eyes meeting Max's with an intensity that made Max's heart skip a beat. "I'm someone you've always known. Even if you don't remember."

Max's pulse quickened, a strange sense of recognition flickering at the edges of his mind. But before he could ask anything more, another memory began to unfold, pulling him deeper into the past.

***

Max stood in the hallway, just outside the room they had once planned to turn into a nursery. The air felt heavy, like the walls themselves were holding their breath. The walls were still bare, the crib they had talked about never bought. It was as if the room itself had become a monument to their unfulfilled dreams, a place they avoided, but one that held all the hopes they'd once had. He stared at the empty space, his heart heavy with the weight of what could have been.

Eve stood beside him, her hand resting lightly on his arm. She was barely holding herself together, her face pale, her eyes dull with the exhaustion of everything they had been through. They had just returned from the doctor's office, the news still fresh in their minds. It was over. There would be no child. No family. No future built on the dreams they had once shared.

Max couldn't speak. He didn't know how to comfort her when he felt so lost himself. The silence between them was thick, almost suffocating.

"We should let it go," Eve said softly, her voice barely audible. She didn't look at him when she spoke, her gaze fixed on the empty room in front of them. The words felt final, like a quiet surrender to a battle they had already lost.

Max swallowed hard, his throat tight with emotion. "I don't know if I can." The words slipped out before he could stop them, and in that moment, he realized how much he had been holding on to, how deeply he had believed that if they just tried harder, if they just fought a little more, they could still have the life they wanted.

Eve turned to him, her eyes filled with love and sadness. "We have to, Max. We can't keep holding on to something that isn't meant to be."

Max closed his eyes, a tear slipping down his cheek. He knew she was right, but the pain of that loss, the weight of what they could never have, was more than he could bear.

It was like carrying the weight of a broken promise, a future that had dissolved before their eyes.

Max blinked back to the present, his heart aching with the memory. They had given up that day. They had let go of the dream of having a child, but the pain of that loss had never really gone away. It had festered, become part of the guilt and fear that had driven Max to try to control everything.

Eli's Compassion

Eli's voice was soft, but it carried a weight that made Max's chest tighten. "It wasn't the life you imagined. But it wasn't the end, either."

Max swallowed hard, his throat tight. "I thought it was. I thought I had failed her."

Eli's gaze softened, and for the briefest moment, there was something almost tender in his eyes. "You didn't fail, Max. You just couldn't see what was meant to be."

Max frowned, confusion flickering through him. "What are you talking about?"

Eli didn't answer directly, but there was something in his expression—something familiar and distant all at once. "You'll understand soon enough."

Chapter 28: Time Slipping Away

The truck rumbled along the empty highway, the quiet hum of the engine filling the space between Max and Eli. The darkness outside seemed to grow deeper as they drove, the world around them narrowing to the small, enclosed bubble of the truck's cab. Max could feel the weight of everything pressing down on him—the memories, the guilt, the losses that had shaped his life. And now, with Eli beside him, guiding him through each step of his past, he couldn't escape the feeling that he was heading toward something inevitable.

The clock on the dash continued its relentless flashing, the numbers 10:32 blinking in and out, casting an odd glow in the dimly lit cab. Max had barely noticed it before, but now, with everything Eli had said and everything that had come back to him in the last few hours, the flashing seemed to pulse in time with the beats of his racing heart.

Max's eyes drifted toward the clock on the dash, still flashing 10:32 in its rhythmic, unrelenting pulse. For years, it had been stuck like that—blinking in and out as though the universe itself was caught in a loop, never able to move forward. It seemed absurd that something as small as a broken clock could hold any significance, but in the stillness of the truck, it was all Max could hear. The silent rhythm synced with his heartbeat, with every thought that ran through his mind. Each blink was a reminder of something undone, something unresolved. Time had stopped for him a long time ago, hadn't it?

How long had it been since he truly felt like his life was moving forward, instead of being stuck in the past? The loss of his mother, the child they never had, Eve's illness—each event had been like a hand gripping the clock, stopping it in place. And now, here he was, watching the same numbers blink back at him, waiting for something—anything—to change.

Eli's voice cut through the silence, his tone light but edged with something more. "You know, you should really get that clock fixed. It's been stuck on 10:32 this whole time. Makes you wonder if time's trying to tell you something."

Max blinked, his gaze shifting to the clock. He hadn't paid much attention to it, but now, as he looked at the steady, flashing numbers, something stirred in his memory—a distant echo from a time long past.

10:32.

"What's 172 times 6, Maxwell Hamblen?" The teacher's voice rang in his mind, pulling him back to that long-forgotten moment in the classroom, where he had first locked eyes with Eve, where everything had begun.

He hadn't known the answer then. But now it felt like the answer had followed him through every step of his life, an invisible tether that had led him to this moment.

Max exhaled, a strange sense of unease settling over him. "I don't know if I believe in signs."

Eli chuckled softly, his eyes twinkling with a mix of humor and something deeper. "Maybe not. But clocks tend to keep time for a reason. And when they stop, well, sometimes that's when you're supposed to start paying attention."

Max frowned, glancing at Eli. There was something in the man's voice, something playful but knowing, as though he understood more than he was letting on.

"What's with the clock, anyway?" Max asked, his voice rough. "It's been stuck like that for years. Just never got around to fixing it."

Eli shrugged, a smile tugging at the corner of his lips. "Maybe it's not about fixing it. Maybe it's about what happens when it finally moves forward."

Max's chest tightened, the weight of those words settling over him like a heavy blanket. He didn't know what Eli was trying to say—at least, not fully—but there was a sense that something was coming, something he couldn't quite grasp yet.

Max couldn't shake the growing suspicion that there was more to Eli than what met the eye. The way the man spoke, the things he seemed to know—how could Eli know about the broken clock or the way Max had always tried to fix things? There was something in Eli's voice, something familiar yet foreign, as though Eli had been with Max through every step of his life, watching from the shadows.

Max glanced sideways at Eli, his mind spinning with questions he couldn't quite bring himself to ask. Who was he really? A friend? A guide? Or something else?

And then there were the little things. The way Eli seemed so calm, so sure. The way his words seemed to pierce right through Max's defenses. It was as though Eli wasn't really here at all—like he was more of an idea, a reflection of something buried deep inside Max's own mind.

Max shivered, despite the warmth in the truck. "Who are you?" Max's voice barely broke the silence.

Eli just smiled, the corners of his mouth tugging upward in a way that made Max's chest tighten. "I'm someone you've always known."

***

Max stood in his father's old workshop, the familiar scent of sawdust and varnish filling the air. It had always been a place of comfort for him, a place where he could escape the chaos of the world outside. But tonight, the workshop felt different. The tools on the wall, the half-finished projects, the workbench—they all seemed frozen in time, waiting for him to make a decision he couldn't take back.

Max could still smell the sawdust, the faint scent of wood varnish that always clung to the air in his father's workshop. As a boy, Max had spent countless hours there, watching his father's hands move with practiced precision, shaping raw materials into something solid, something real. His father had always told him, "Steady hands, Max. Things worth having take time."

But time was the one thing Max had never seemed to have enough of. Not when his mother had gotten sick. Not when the doctor told him and Eve they couldn't have children.

And especially not when Eve's diagnosis had come, like a hammer splitting the life they had built in two.

He thought of how his father had never rushed, had never forced anything. Max had tried to emulate that patience in the beginning, but as life grew more complicated, he'd become desperate to control everything—to fix everything. That's where he'd gone wrong. He had tried to speed up the process, to mold life into the shape he needed it to be, but life wasn't something you could sculpt with steady hands.

He had learned that too late.

The duffel bag sat on the floor by the door, packed and ready. Inside was everything he thought he needed to save Eve—to fix what was broken. The bank robbery had been a desperate plan, born from the fear of losing her, from the helplessness that had gnawed at him for months. He had convinced himself that if he could just get enough money, if he could just buy her more time, then everything would be okay.

But now, standing in the workshop, his hands trembling with the weight of what he was about to do, Max wasn't so sure. He looked down at the bag, his heart pounding in his chest. This wasn't who he was. He wasn't a criminal. He wasn't someone who could walk into a bank, wave a gun around, and demand money. But for Eve—for the chance to save her—he was willing to do anything.

His father's voice echoed in his mind, a memory from long ago. You're building something bigger than you know, Max. Steady hands. Don't rush it. Things worth having take time.

Max swallowed hard, his throat tight. He hadn't built anything. He had tried, time and again, but everything he had touched seemed to fall apart. His father had built things that lasted, things that stood the test of time. But Max? All he had were broken promises and a future that was slipping away.

"I'm sorry, Dad," Max whispered, his voice breaking.

He grabbed the duffel bag and walked out of the workshop, leaving behind the life he had tried so hard to build.

The memory hit Max hard, the weight of that decision pressing down on him even now. It had been the moment when everything had truly started to unravel. He had convinced himself that robbing the bank was the only way to save Eve, the only way to control the chaos that had taken over their lives. But in doing so, he had lost sight of what really mattered.

"I thought I could fix it," Max muttered, his voice heavy with regret. "I thought I could make it all right."

Eli's gaze was steady, but there was a softness in his eyes that Max hadn't noticed before. "You thought you could control it. But some things were never yours to control."

Max exhaled, the truth of those words settling over him like a lead weight. He had spent so long trying to control the uncontrollable—his mother's death, the child they couldn't have, Eve's illness. And in his desperation, he had lost sight of the love that had been right in front of him.

"What if I never stop running?" Max asked, his voice barely above a whisper. "What if I never figure out how to let go?"

Eli smiled gently, a knowing glint in his eyes. "You will. Maybe not all at once. But you will."

Max glanced at him, something flickering at the edges of his mind—something about Eli that he couldn't quite grasp, but that felt familiar in a way he couldn't explain.

He opened his mouth to ask another question, but before he could, another memory surfaced, pulling him under.

***

Max and Eve sat in his old pickup truck, driving down a long stretch of country road. It was one of the last good days they had shared together, before everything had started to spiral out of control. Eve sat beside him, her hand resting lightly on his leg, her eyes focused on the horizon ahead.

The memory came flooding back, vivid and full of sensory detail. Max could still feel the warmth of the late afternoon sun against his skin, the way the light had turned the fields golden as they drove down that long stretch of road. Eve's hand rested on his thigh, her fingers warm and familiar, a connection that had always grounded him. The wind blew through the open windows, carrying with it the smell of grass and earth, the sounds of birds calling from the fields.

It had been one of those rare moments when everything felt right, when the world had slowed down just enough for them to catch their breath. They had talked about the future that day—the kind of conversations that had once filled their lives with hope. But there had been a weight to

Eve's words, a sense of finality that Max hadn't wanted to acknowledge.

"I'm scared, Max," Eve had said, her voice barely above a whisper. The vulnerability in her voice had pierced him, a reminder that no matter how hard he tried to protect her, there were some things even love couldn't shield her from.

"I know," he had whispered back, gripping the steering wheel as if it were the only thing keeping him tethered to the present. "But I'll be with you. No matter what."

That promise had felt so solid, so unbreakable, in the golden light of that day. But now, looking back, Max wasn't sure if it had been enough.

Eve smiled, her eyes filled with love. "That's all I need."
The memory faded, but the ache in Max's chest remained. That had been one of the last times they had talked about the future, about the life they had imagined but would never have. And now, sitting here in the truck with Eli, Max felt the weight of those lost dreams pressing down on him.

Eli's voice broke through the silence once again, quiet but filled with meaning. "You gave her everything she needed, Max. Even if you couldn't see it."

Max's heart pounded, the truth of those words cutting deep. He had spent so long believing that he had failed her, that he hadn't been enough. But now, with Eli's steady presence beside him, he was starting to see the cracks in that belief.

The clock on the dash flashed again, 10:32 blinking steadily in the dim light.

"You think the clock will move forward someday?" Max asked, his voice filled with something close to hope.

Eli smiled, his eyes glinting with a quiet understanding. "Maybe. When the time is right."

Chapter 29: Ghosts of What Might Have Been

The truck rolled on through the night, the steady hum of the engine the only sound breaking the silence. The road ahead was a void, swallowed by shadows, as if the night itself had a weight that pressed against the truck, enclosing it in an endless darkness. The faint gleam of the headlights barely illuminated the stretch of asphalt before them, swallowed almost as quickly as it appeared. The trees lining the highway were no more than black silhouettes, their branches twisting in unnatural shapes, like silent watchers of a journey that felt destined for something unknown. Max could feel the hum of the engine vibrating through his hands on the wheel, the only real, tangible thing left in a night that seemed to pull him further from reality and deeper into his own mind.

Max's thoughts felt heavy, weighed down by the memories that Eli had drawn out of him over the past hours. Each memory that surfaced felt like a stone being dropped into deep water, rippling outward, breaking the stillness of the surface, but never sinking completely out of sight. The weight of them pulled at Max, making it hard to focus on the road ahead. He could feel them pressing against his chest, tightening his breath, like they were building into something he wasn't ready to face. Each piece of his past was clearer now, sharper, as if someone had taken the blurred edges of forgotten moments and brought them into painful focus. The past was no longer distant; it was right there with him, sitting in the truck, occupying the space between him and Eli.

But beneath it all, there was still something gnawing at him. The feeling that no matter how much he remembered, how much he accepted, there was still something missing. Something he couldn't quite grasp.

Eli had grown quieter as they drove, but his presence was as steady as ever. Max could feel him there, like a guide leading him toward something just out of reach.

"There's something more, isn't there?" Max asked, his voice low. "Something I'm not seeing."

Eli glanced at him, a small smile tugging at his lips. "You're close."

Max frowned, the weight of Eli's words settling over him. There had been a growing sense of familiarity about Eli, something that had been building since the moment they met. But Max still couldn't put his finger on it, still couldn't shake the feeling that there was a piece of the puzzle he was missing.

And then, as if pulled by an invisible thread, his mind drifted back to the clock on the dash. The clock had been flashing for hours now—10:32, over and over, each flicker a silent reminder of something that tugged at the edges of Max's consciousness. It wasn't just a malfunction anymore. It was as if time itself had stopped for him, caught in an endless loop. That small digital display had become more than a broken clock—it was a symbol, a signal, pulsing with an urgency that Max couldn't quite understand but could feel deep in his bones. Every time the numbers blinked in and out, it was like a heartbeat, a reminder that something was left unresolved, something hanging in the balance.

Eli had joked about the clock earlier, and it had seemed like nothing more than an offhand comment. But now, as Max stared at the flashing numbers, something stirred deep inside him—a memory he had long buried.

***

Max sat at his desk in the classroom, staring blankly at the chalkboard as the teacher's voice droned on in the background. The classroom had always been a place where Max felt like he didn't quite fit. The walls, once covered in colorful posters, now seemed to close in on him. The fluorescent lights overhead buzzed faintly, casting a sterile glow on the rows of desks, making everything feel distant, cold. But when his eyes drifted toward Eve, sitting just a few seats away, the world softened. She had this way of making everything feel less overwhelming. Her presence was like sunlight breaking through clouds, warming the cold spaces in his life. And even when he was lost in thought, distracted by the daydream of a life where things made sense, just a glimpse of her smile could bring him back, grounding him in something real, something hopeful.

He wasn't paying attention—his mind was elsewhere, focused on the girl sitting a few desks away.

Eve.

He had always been drawn to her, even when they were kids. There was something about her that made everything else seem distant, unimportant. And even though he didn't fully understand it yet, he knew she was special. She always had been.

"Maxwell Hamblen," the teacher called out, snapping Max from his thoughts. "What's 172 times 6?"

The classroom had erupted in soft laughter, and Max had felt his face flush with embarrassment. He had no idea what the answer was. Math had never been his strong suit, and he hadn't been paying attention anyway.

But Eve had smiled at him, that warm, understanding smile she always gave him. And in that moment, the embarrassment had faded, replaced by something else— something that made him feel like maybe he wasn't alone.

The memory faded, but the feeling lingered. Max's heart pounded in his chest as he stared at the flashing clock. 10:32. The answer to the math problem from so long ago.

He hadn't known it then, but that moment had stayed with him, etched into the fabric of his life in ways he hadn't realized until now.

"You see it now, don't you?" Eli's voice was soft, but there was an edge to it, as if he knew exactly what Max was thinking.

Max swallowed hard, his throat tight. "The clock. It's been stuck at 10:32 this whole time."

Eli nodded, his expression unreadable. "Funny how time works, isn't it? Sometimes it feels like it's standing still. Other times, like it's slipping away faster than you can hold on to."

Max's chest tightened, the weight of those words sinking in. Time had always felt slippery to him—ever since Eve had gotten sick, ever since he had tried so hard to fix everything. It had felt like no matter how hard he tried, he was always running out of time.

"What does it mean?" Max asked, his voice trembling. "Why does the clock matter?"

Eli's gaze softened, and for the first time, there was something close to sympathy in his eyes. "It's a reminder, Max. Of the moments you can't go back to. Of the choices you made. And of the ones you didn't."

Max felt his breath hitch, the truth of those words hitting him like a punch to the gut. He had spent so long trying to control time, to fix what had already passed, that he hadn't seen the moments that truly mattered slipping through his fingers.

And now, with the clock flashing 10:32 in the background, Max felt the weight of everything he had tried to outrun finally catching up to him.

***

Max and Eve stood together in their small living room, the weight of the doctor's words still heavy in the air around them. The news had been hard to hear—the final confirmation that they would never have the child they had dreamed of, the family they had hoped for.

Eve's eyes were red, her face pale from crying, but there was a quiet strength in her that Max had always admired. She had always been the one who could handle the hard truths, even when he couldn't.

"We have to let it go, Max," Eve said softly, her voice breaking. "We can't keep holding on to something that isn't going to happen."

But letting go hadn't been easy. It was like trying to release something that had woven itself into the very fibers of their lives. That dream of a child, of building a family, had been more than just a hope—it had been a part of who they were, part of the foundation they had built their love on. And when they were forced to let it go, it wasn't just the dream that was lost. It was pieces of themselves, pieces they hadn't even known were there until they were gone. Max could still feel the echoes of that loss, the way it had hollowed him out, leaving an emptiness that nothing else could fill. Even after all these years, the weight of it lingered, pulling at him, reminding him of what could have been.

Max had nodded, but his heart had felt like it was being crushed under the weight of their lost dreams. He had wanted to fight, to keep pushing for a solution, for some way to make everything right. But Eve had been right—they couldn't keep holding on to something that was slipping away.

They had let go that day. Of the dream of having a child. Of the life they had imagined together. And though they had moved forward, a part of Max had never stopped grieving for what could have been.

The memory faded, and Max blinked back to the present, his hands trembling on the steering wheel. He had tried so hard to fix everything, to control the outcomes of his life. But some things couldn't be fixed. Some things had to be accepted.

And now, sitting here in the truck, with Eli beside him, Max felt the weight of that acceptance settling over him like a blanket. It wasn't about fixing things. It was about being present. About letting go.

"You couldn't have known," Eli said quietly, as if sensing Max's thoughts. "But maybe now you're ready to understand."

Max turned to him, his chest tight. "Who are you, Eli?"

Eli's smile was soft, almost sad. "You already know."

Max's heart skipped a beat, the flicker of recognition flashing in his mind. He didn't understand it fully—not yet—but there was something in Eli's presence that felt so familiar. Something that had been with him all along.

And as he glanced back at the flashing clock, 10:32 blinking steadily in the dim light, Max knew that time was running out. But for the first time, he wasn't afraid.

Eli's voice was calm, filled with quiet understanding. "You're almost there, Max. You're almost ready."

Max exhaled, his heart pounding. "Ready for what?"

Eli's smile deepened, his eyes filled with something Max couldn't quite name. "To finally let go."

Chapter 30: The Weight of Time

The truck's tires hummed along the road, the darkness outside seeming to press in from all directions. Max could barely see beyond the beams of the headlights, which cut through the inky blackness like a thin blade. It felt as if the world outside had ceased to exist, swallowed whole by the night. Only the truck's cabin remained, a small island of existence in an otherwise empty void. And inside that small world, Max felt the weight of everything he had been running from, every secret, every loss, slowly closing in on him.

The flashing clock on the dash—10:32—seemed to blink in time with his heartbeat, a steady, relentless pulse that pulled at his attention. The soft red glow cast an eerie light inside the truck, highlighting the tension in Max's clenched jaw, the lines of worry etched deep into his face. His hands gripped the steering wheel tightly, knuckles even paler from the strain. He was driving, but the destination no longer seemed important. He wasn't sure where he was heading or what he was supposed to find at the end of this road.

Eli sat beside him, silent but ever-present, his gaze fixed forward, as though he was looking far beyond the road, seeing things that Max couldn't. The air between them felt thick, charged with the weight of unspoken truths, of realizations Max wasn't ready to face. Eli had become more than just a passenger. He was a guide, a figure who seemed to know Max's inner workings better than he did himself.

"Why had Eli pointed out the stupid clock?" Max muttered under his breath. He shifted uncomfortably in his seat, glancing once more at the numbers—10:32, still blinking like a heartbeat. "This thing's been blinking for years, and I never could fix it… now I can't stop looking at it."

The thought gnawed at him. Why now? Why, after all this time, had the broken clock become something more? Something he couldn't ignore. He had lived with its blinking for so long that it had become part of the truck itself, part of him. But now, every flash felt like a call, a reminder of something just out of reach.

Max's thoughts churned, a storm of memories and emotions swirling together, pulling him deeper into himself. Eli's presence had always been steady, a quiet force by his side, but now it felt like something more—like Eli was waiting for something. A part of Max knew this moment had been coming all along, but he had been avoiding it, running from it. Yet there was no escape anymore. The time was coming. He could feel it in his bones.

Eli finally broke the silence, his voice soft yet resonant, as if he knew exactly what Max was thinking. "You've always been running."

Max swallowed hard, his throat tight. He kept his gaze on the road ahead, but the darkness beyond the headlights seemed to mirror the darkness inside him. "I didn't know how to stop," he admitted, the words coming out in a hoarse whisper, as if they had been buried too deep for too long.

Eli nodded, his gaze still focused on the road, but his voice carried a weight that made Max's chest tighten. "You were always trying to control what you couldn't. Always trying to fix things that were out of your hands."

Max exhaled slowly, the truth of those words settling over him like a shroud. He had spent his entire life trying to control the uncontrollable—his mother's death when he was just a boy, the endless struggle with Eve's illness, the child they had never been able to have. Each loss had driven him deeper into himself, each failure had made him more desperate to fix the next thing, to make things right. But no matter how hard he tried, it had all slipped through his fingers, like water running down a drain.

"I thought I had to," Max admitted, his voice barely above a whisper. "I thought if I didn't, I'd lose everything."

Eli finally turned to look at him, his eyes filled with a quiet understanding that made Max's heart ache. "And now that you've lost it," Eli asked, his voice gentle but probing, "what do you have left?"

Max's chest tightened. That was the question he had been avoiding for so long. He had lost everything that mattered—Eve, the dreams they had shared, the life they had tried to build together. And now, all that was left was the guilt, the crushing weight of knowing that no matter how hard he had tried, he hadn't been able to save her. He had failed her.

But there was something else. Something he wasn't ready to face yet, though he could feel it looming just out of sight, waiting for him to confront it.

The clock on the dash flashed again—10:32, always the same. The numbers blinked steadily in the dim light, like a pulse that refused to be ignored.

"You're still trying to fix it," Eli said, his voice firm but not unkind. "Still trying to make sense of it all."

Max glanced at him, confusion flickering through his mind. "What do you mean?"

Eli's smile was soft, almost sad. "You're holding on to something that isn't there. You're trying to control something you never had control over."

Max's heart pounded, the truth of those words cutting deep. He had spent so long trying to control his life, to fix what had gone wrong, to make things right. But in the end, all of his efforts had only pushed him further away from what truly mattered. He had been so focused on controlling the outcome that he had forgotten to live in the moment, to cherish the time he had with Eve while he still had it.

"What was I supposed to do?" Max asked, his voice thick with emotion. "Just let it all fall apart?"

Eli's gaze softened, and for the briefest moment, there was something in his eyes that made Max's chest tighten—a flicker of something familiar, something he couldn't quite place. "Sometimes, things have to fall apart so they can come back together."

Max didn't know how to respond. The weight of everything he had lost, everything he had tried so hard to hold on to, felt like it was pressing down on him, suffocating him. He had spent so long trying to hold everything together, to control the chaos of life, that he hadn't realized the toll it had taken on him. And on Eve.

But there was something else. Something that had been there all along, just beyond his reach, waiting for him to see it.

Eli's voice was quiet, almost a whisper. "You're closer than you think, Max. Closer to understanding what this is all about."

Max's pulse quickened, a strange sense of anticipation building inside him. He didn't know what Eli meant, but he could feel it—the weight of the moment, the sense that everything was leading to something he couldn't yet see. The pieces were slowly coming together, but the final picture remained just out of focus.

And then, another memory began to surface, pulling him back into the past.

***

Max and Eve sat together on the couch, the dim light of the living room casting long shadows across the walls. The air felt thick, heavy with the weight of their unspoken grief.

It had been weeks since they had received the news—the final confirmation that they would never have the child they had dreamed of. Weeks of silence, of living in a house that felt emptier with each passing day.

The silence between them was thick, heavy with unspoken pain. Max hadn't known what to say. He had tried to comfort Eve, tried to tell her that they would find a way to move forward, but the words had felt hollow, empty. Each sentence fell flat, a pale imitation of hope that neither of them truly believed.

"We should've had a life with a child," Eve said quietly, her voice breaking the stillness. Her eyes, normally so full of life, now held a deep sadness that tore at Max's heart. "We could've been happy."

Max swallowed hard, his throat tight. "I know."

Eve's gaze was distant, focused on a spot across the room. Max followed her line of sight to the corner where they had once imagined placing a crib. It was an empty space now, a place where their dreams had once lived, but now, only the echo of what could have been remained.

"I think about it all the time," Eve whispered, her voice trembling. "What it would've been like. What kind of life we would've had."

Max closed his eyes, the weight of her words crushing him. He had thought about it too—endlessly. He had imagined their life together, raising a child, building the family they had always wanted. But those dreams had died the day they got the news. And yet, even after all these years, the loss still haunted him.

"I'm sorry," Max whispered, his voice trembling. "I'm so sorry."

Eve turned to him, her eyes filled with love and sadness. She reached out, her hand brushing against his cheek, wiping away the tear that had slipped down his face. "It wasn't your fault, Max. It wasn't something you could control."

Max shook his head, tears slipping down his cheeks. "But I wanted to give you that. I wanted to give you everything."

Eve smiled through her tears, her hand reaching out to touch his face, her touch soft and warm, like the gentle caress of a summer breeze. "You gave me more than enough. You gave me you."

The memory faded, leaving Max breathless, his heart pounding in his chest. That moment—the loss of their child, the life they would never have—had shaped everything that had come after. It had driven him to the edge, made him desperate to fix what couldn't be fixed. The guilt had consumed him, pushing him further from Eve and the life they had still been able to share.

But now, with Eli beside him, Max was starting to see things differently.

"You're still holding on to that loss," Eli said softly, his voice filled with understanding. "Still trying to make sense of what could have been."

Max swallowed hard, his throat tight with emotion. "I don't know how to let go of it."

Eli smiled gently, his eyes filled with something Max couldn't quite name. "Maybe it's not about letting go. Maybe it's about seeing what's still here."

Max blinked, confusion flickering through him. "What do you mean?"

Eli didn't answer right away. He simply stared out at the road ahead, his expression thoughtful. "You'll understand soon enough."

Max's chest tightened, the sense of familiarity with Eli growing stronger. There was something about him, something that felt so close, like a whisper of a memory Max couldn't quite grasp.
And then, as if on cue, the clock on the dash flashed again—10:32.

Max stared at the numbers, his heart pounding. The significance of that time, the connection to the moment in the classroom when he had first locked eyes with Eve—it was all coming together. But there was still something missing.

"You always wanted a family," Eli said quietly, his voice soft but edged with meaning. "And you never stopped grieving for the one you lost."

Max swallowed hard, his chest tight. "I couldn't let it go. It felt like I failed her."

Eli's smile was gentle, almost sad. "But what if you didn't fail? What if you gave her everything she needed?"

Max blinked, his mind racing. He had spent so long believing that he had failed Eve, that he hadn't been enough. But now, with Eli beside him, guiding him through the memories of his life, he was starting to see that maybe he had been enough. Maybe his love, his presence, had been all that Eve had needed.

And then, something shifted. A thought that had been lingering at the edges of his mind for so long suddenly clicked into place.

Max turned to Eli, his heart pounding. "Who are you?"

Eli's smile deepened, his eyes filled with a quiet, knowing light. "You already know, Max."

Max's breath caught in his throat. The familiarity, the sense of connection—it all rushed to the surface, overwhelming him. He didn't understand it fully, but he could feel the truth hovering just out of reach.

Eli's voice was soft, filled with understanding. "You're almost ready, Max. Almost ready to see what this has all been about."

Max exhaled, his chest tight. "What's going to happen?"

Eli smiled gently, his eyes filled with something Max couldn't quite place. "You'll see. Soon."

Chapter 31: The Final Turn

The road stretched endlessly ahead, the dark ribbon of asphalt cutting through the night like a scar across the landscape. The air was still, heavy with the kind of quiet that felt like it was waiting for something to happen. The hum of the truck's engine was a constant, lulling rhythm that seemed to blend into the very pulse of Max's thoughts, the vibration beneath his hands on the steering wheel grounding him in the present, even as his mind churned with memories of the past.

The truck's headlights sliced through the darkness, illuminating nothing but an empty stretch of highway that seemed to go on forever. Max drove in silence, his mind still reeling from everything Eli had guided him through. He had faced his deepest fears, the memories he had buried, and the losses he had tried so hard to control. And yet, there was something more—something he hadn't quite grasped, like a shadow lurking just beyond his reach.

The clock on the dash continued its steady blinking, 10:32 flashing in the dim light. Each pulse of the clock felt like a heartbeat, slow and methodical, ticking in time with the weight in Max's chest. Time had been frozen, stuck in that single moment, just as Max had been stuck in his guilt, his need to fix what couldn't be fixed.

Eli sat beside him, quiet but ever-present. There was something different in his demeanor now, a calmness that hadn't been there before, as if the tension between them had finally eased, as if Eli had been waiting for this moment all along. Max could feel the weight of what was coming, the sense that everything was building to a final, inevitable conclusion.

"You've been carrying this weight for a long time," Eli said softly, his voice cutting through the silence like a thread that pulled at the edges of Max's thoughts. "But you're almost there."

Max nodded, his chest tight with emotion. He knew what Eli meant. He had spent so long running from the truth, from the reality of what had happened, that he hadn't even realized how heavy the burden had become. But now, with Eli guiding him, he could feel the final pieces falling into place, the edges of the puzzle that had eluded him for so long finally starting to take shape.

"I don't know if I'm ready," Max admitted, his voice trembling. The vulnerability in his words felt like a crack in the armor he had spent years building, and the fear that had been gnawing at him for so long suddenly felt exposed, raw. "I don't know if I can let go."

Eli smiled gently, his eyes filled with understanding, as if he had heard those words before, from someone else. "You don't have to be ready," Eli said, his tone steady but soft, like a lullaby whispered in the dark. "You just have to be willing."

Max swallowed hard, his throat tight. The fear of what was coming, of the truth he had been avoiding, gnawed at him like a predator circling in the shadows. He could feel it closing in, and yet there was no turning back now. He had come too far, and the end was almost here.

As they drove, the landscape began to change in subtle, almost imperceptible ways. The horizon seemed to blur, the edges of the world softening, as if reality itself was fading, unraveling like a thread pulled too tight. The trees along the roadside bent and twisted in the wind, their silhouettes stretching out into the night, growing darker and more indistinct with each passing mile. Max felt a strange sense of detachment, like he was drifting between two worlds—the one he had known and the one that was waiting for him just beyond the veil.

Eli remained silent, his presence a quiet comfort beside Max. But Max could feel it—the sense that Eli knew more than he was letting on. The familiarity, the connection that

Max still couldn't fully understand, but that had been with him all along.

And then, as if on cue, the memories began to surface again—moments from his life that had shaped everything, that had led him to this point. They flickered in his mind like scenes from an old film, the edges of the images blurred and worn, but the emotions still sharp, still real.

***

Max sat beside Eve's hospital bed, the steady beep of the monitors filling the room with a soft, rhythmic pulse. The sterile smell of antiseptic hung in the air, a sharp contrast to the warmth that still lingered in Eve's eyes as she looked at him. Her body was weak, frail, but her spirit—her heart —was still as strong as it had ever been. Her smile was gentle, a quiet reassurance that everything would be okay, even if he couldn't see how.

Max held her hand in his, the weight of it so light now, as if she were already slipping away, like sand through his fingers. He couldn't hold on tight enough, no matter how hard he tried.

"I'm sorry," Max whispered, his voice breaking under the strain of everything he hadn't been able to do. His throat was tight, the words heavy with guilt. "I'm so sorry I couldn't do more."

Eve shook her head slowly, her smile never fading, though her eyes were tired, as if the weight of the world had finally caught up to her. "You did everything, Max. You've always done everything."

Max blinked back tears, his heart aching in a way that felt too big for his chest. "But I couldn't save you."

Eve's eyes softened, her gaze filled with love and something else—something that made Max's heart twist. "I never needed you to save me," she said, her voice so soft it was almost a breath. "I just needed you to be with me."

Max closed his eyes, the weight of her words pressing down on him like a tidal wave. He had spent so long trying to fix everything, trying to control the uncontrollable, as if by sheer force of will he could keep her here, keep everything from slipping away. But in the end, all Eve had needed was for him to be there, to love her in the way that only he could.

"I love you," Max whispered, his voice trembling with the weight of everything he couldn't say.

"I love you too," Eve replied, her voice barely above a whisper, but the emotion in it was as deep and steady as the ocean. "Always."

She had wanted so much for them—for their life together, for the family they had dreamed of. But she had never blamed him for what they couldn't have. She had never held him responsible for the things that had been out of their control.

And now, in her final moments, all she wanted was for him to understand that he had been enough. That his love had been everything she had ever needed.

The memory faded like a dream dissolving in the morning light, and Max was back in the truck, his heart heavy with the weight of what had been. He had loved Eve, and she had loved him. That had been enough. And yet, there was still something more, something he hadn't quite faced.

The clock on the dash blinked again—10:32. Always the same. The numbers seemed to pulse in time with his heartbeat, steady and relentless, as if the clock itself was waiting for him to catch up, to understand.

"You're almost there, Max," Eli said quietly, his voice a gentle whisper in the darkness. "Almost ready to see what this has all been about."

Max exhaled slowly, his chest tight. "What is this? What's happening?"

Eli's smile deepened, and for the first time, there was something almost otherworldly in his eyes, something that made Max's skin prickle with the sense that he was standing on the edge of something vast and unknowable. "You already know."

Max's heart pounded, the sense of recognition flickering at the edges of his mind like the faint glow of a distant star. He had been running from the truth for so long, but now, with Eli guiding him, he could feel it—the truth waiting just beyond the horizon, ready to reveal itself.

The truck seemed to slow, though Max couldn't remember easing off the gas. The world around them faded into a soft, golden light, the edges of reality blurring as if they were driving into a dream. Max felt a strange sense of peace wash over him, the weight of his guilt, his fear, slowly lifting, like a weight he had carried for so long that he had forgotten what it felt like to be without it.

"You've carried this for long enough," Eli said, his voice filled with quiet understanding. "It's time to let go."

Max swallowed hard, his throat tight. "What if I can't?"

Eli's eyes softened, and he reached out, placing a hand on Max's shoulder, the gesture so simple yet so full of meaning. "You can. You've already started."

Max blinked, his vision blurring with unshed tears. The weight of everything—the loss, the pain, the guilt—was still there, but it felt lighter now. More bearable.

And then, in the quiet stillness, Max felt it—an overwhelming sense of familiarity, of connection. Eli had been with him this entire time, guiding him through every step of his journey. But now, as they approached the end, Max could see it clearly.

Max's breath caught in his throat, the realization crashing over him like a wave. The connection he had felt, the sense of familiarity—it all made sense now. But even as the understanding settled over him, it wasn't complete. There was still something just beyond his reach, something important that hadn't yet revealed itself.

The weight on his chest didn't disappear. It lingered, heavy and insistent, reminding him that this journey wasn't over yet.

Eli sat beside him, silent, his eyes watching Max carefully. There was no rush in the way Eli looked at him, no push for answers. It was as if Eli understood that Max needed to take this final turn on his own. To arrive at the truth in his own time.

Max stared at the road ahead, feeling a strange pull in his chest—a tug toward something he couldn't fully grasp. The landscape outside seemed to blur, the darkness folding into itself, swallowing the familiar world whole. But he wasn't scared. Not anymore.

The blinking clock on the dash continued to flash, locked in time at 10:32. Its rhythmic pulse was like a heartbeat, steady, constant, waiting for something. But what?

Max's hands gripped the steering wheel tightly as his thoughts drifted back to Eve—back to her smile, her laughter, the way she had always been his anchor, even when everything around him was falling apart. He could almost hear her voice now, soft and comforting, reminding him of all the things that mattered most.

"You can't fix everything, Max," she had told him once. "But that's not what love is about. It's about being there when it counts."

His heart ached at the memory, but there was something different now. It wasn't just the pain of loss anymore. There was a strange, quiet acceptance blooming in the space where the hurt had lived for so long.

He hadn't been able to fix everything. He hadn't been able to save Eve. But he had loved her. He had been there. And that had to count for something.

Eli shifted beside him, breaking the stillness. "You don't have to carry it all, Max," he said softly. "Not anymore."

Max blinked, his breath shaky. "I've carried it for so long. I don't even know how to let it go."

Eli's gaze remained steady. "You start by realizing you don't need to carry it. Not alone."

Max's chest tightened again, the weight of the past still pressing down on him. He wanted to let go. He wanted to move forward, to find some measure of peace. But the fear of losing everything—of not being enough—still clung to him like a shadow.

As the truck rolled through the endless night, Max's mind kept circling back to that thought. The things he couldn't fix. The promises he couldn't keep. But also the love that had never wavered, even in the darkest moments. The love that had bound him to Eve, to everything they had shared, everything they had lost.

And then, in the quiet stillness of the night, Max finally allowed himself to feel it—to feel the truth of what Eli had been guiding him toward all along. It wasn't about fixing things. It was about letting go of the need to control the uncontrollable. It was about accepting that some things were beyond his reach, beyond his ability to change.

Max closed his eyes for a moment, the tears finally slipping free. For the first time in what felt like forever, he allowed himself to grieve. To mourn the life he had lost, the dreams that had slipped away, the promises he had made but couldn't keep.

And in that grief, there was a strange sense of relief. A release. As if the weight he had been carrying for so long was finally beginning to lift.

When he opened his eyes again, the road ahead seemed clearer, the darkness less suffocating. The clock on the dash still blinked, 10:32, frozen in time. But Max knew now that time wasn't something he could control. And maybe… that was okay.

The truth he had been searching for wasn't about answers or solutions. It wasn't about fixing the past. It was about accepting it. Accepting the love he had shared with Eve, the choices he had made, and the things he couldn't change.

Max's hands relaxed on the wheel, the tension in his body slowly unwinding. The road ahead stretched out before him, endless and unknown, but it didn't feel as daunting as it had before.

Eli's voice broke the silence once more, soft and reassuring. "You're ready now, Max. You've been ready for a long time."

Max exhaled slowly, his chest feeling lighter than it had in years. He didn't know exactly what was waiting for him at the end of this road, but for the first time, he wasn't afraid to find out.

And with that thought, he drove on—into the night, into
the unknown, but no longer running from the past.

317

Chapter 32: The Moment Between Breaths

The world outside the truck had become a blur of golden light, the edges of reality softening like a dream slowly unfurling. Time seemed to stretch and warp, unraveling itself as if the very fabric of existence was loosening its hold. Max could feel it—his chest tightening with the weight of the realization that had been building inside him since Eli first appeared.

The connection he had felt, the strange sense of familiarity—it all made sense now, like the pieces of a puzzle finally falling into place. But even as the final picture began to emerge, there was still something more—something just out of reach, hovering on the edge of his mind, waiting for that last elusive piece to lock into position.

Eli sat quietly beside him, his presence a steady, grounding force in the shifting world around them. But there was a subtle shift now, a ripple in the air, as though everything was about to converge into a single moment of clarity. The golden light outside the truck seemed to thicken, as if reality itself was melting into something new, something greater.

The clock on the dash continued its steady blinking, 10:32, pulsing like a heartbeat. The same moment, frozen in time.

Just as Max had been frozen—locked in his guilt, his need to fix what could never be fixed. That blinking number was more than just time. It was a tether, holding him back, keeping him from moving forward.

Max exhaled slowly, the weight of everything pressing down on him. "What happens now?" he whispered, his voice trembling, barely more than a breath.

Eli's eyes softened, a quiet understanding deep in his gaze. "Now, you let go."

The words were simple, but they hit Max like a wave. Let go. He had been holding on for so long, clutching to the guilt, the pain, the belief that he hadn't done enough—that he hadn't been enough. The thought of letting go felt like stepping off a cliff, into a void. But here, now, with Eli beside him, there was a sense of calm that he hadn't felt in years. As if the world was finally giving him permission to stop.

The golden light outside thickened, almost luminous now, and as Max looked ahead, the road began to shift, blurring and morphing into something familiar. His heart skipped a beat as recognition dawned.

It was the road he and Eve had driven down so many times. The road they had taken on their last ride together, before everything had changed. Before their lives had been split apart by fate, by illness, by things beyond their control.

The truck slowed, not by Max's hand, but as if guided by something unseen—something that knew where it was leading him. Max's hands loosened on the steering wheel, his breath catching in his throat. He wasn't driving anymore. He wasn't in control. And for the first time, he didn't try to fight it. He let the road take him where he needed to go.

***

The memory was vivid now, more real than a dream. Max and Eve, sitting in the old truck, the golden light of the setting sun casting a warm glow over the world around them. The sky had been painted in hues of orange and pink, the colors bleeding together like a watercolor that could never be contained. It was one of those rare moments when everything felt suspended, timeless.

They had taken that drive on a whim, a desperate escape from the suffocating weight of Eve's illness. The doctors had been clear—there wasn't much time left. The treatments weren't working. But for one perfect afternoon, they had allowed themselves to forget. To pretend that the world was still theirs, that the future was still something they could grasp with both hands.

"I wish we could stay like this forever," Eve had whispered, her hand resting on Max's leg, her touch warm, her voice carrying the soft lilt of a secret wish.

Max had smiled, though his heart had ached. The sky, the road, the quiet hum of the truck—it had all felt so painfully beautiful in that moment, like they were driving through a world made just for them. But beneath the beauty, there was a sadness, a quiet acceptance of the inevitable.

"Yeah," Max had replied, his voice thick with emotion. "Me too."

They had driven in silence for a while after that, both of them lost in their own thoughts. There were no words that could bridge the gap between them and what was coming. But in that moment, they had been together. And for a brief, fleeting second, that had been enough.

As they reached the end of the road, the light from the sun seemed to stretch into infinity, casting long shadows that danced across the horizon. Eve had turned to him then, her eyes filled with unshed tears, her smile soft but trembling.

"Promise me something," she had said, her voice barely above a whisper.

Max's chest had tightened, the weight of her words already settling into his bones. He had nodded, not trusting himself to speak.

"When it's over… when I'm gone…" She had faltered, her voice breaking, but she had pressed on. "Don't carry this with you forever. Don't let it keep you from living."

Max had swallowed hard, his throat constricting. The air between them had felt thick, heavy with the unspoken truth. "I don't know if I can do that."

Eve had smiled then, her tears finally spilling over, glistening in the dying light of the sun. "You can. You're stronger than you think."

Present: Their Final Breaths

The memory dissolved, and Max was back in the truck, but the ache in his chest remained. The weight of everything— the loss, the guilt, the promises he had made and broken—

it all pressed down on him. But there was something else now. A flicker of light, a sense of release.

Max lay on the cold floor of the bank, his breath coming in shallow, ragged gasps. The world around him had faded into a dull hum, his vision blurred, the edges of reality darkening. Blood pooled beneath him, seeping into the cracks in the tile, the pain from the bullet wound radiating through his chest with every heartbeat. He could feel himself slipping away, the darkness pulling him under.

And yet, somewhere far away, in a sterile hospital room, Eve lay in her bed, her breaths slow and labored, her body weak and fragile. The heart monitor beside her beeped steadily, each sound marking the passage of time, ticking down the final moments of her life. She could feel it too— the pull, the quiet, inevitable pull toward something else.

Max's thoughts swam, disjointed memories flashing before him like broken pieces of glass. Eve's smile, her laughter, the way she had held him when everything else had fallen apart. He could feel her now, closer than ever, as if she were right there beside him.

In the hospital room, the golden light filtered through the window, soft and warm, wrapping Eve in its glow. A shadowy figure stood at her side, his hand gently resting on hers, a touch that was both comforting and familiar.

"Max will be okay," the figure whispered, his voice soft and filled with quiet reassurance. "You can let go now."

Eve's chest rose and fell with one final breath, her body sinking deeper into the bed as the heart monitor flatlined beside her. The steady beep faded into a long, continuous tone, signaling the end.

And across town, in a cold, blood-soaked bank, Max's breath hitched, his chest rising one final time before everything went still. His eyes, glassy and unfocused, fixed on the clock on the wall—the last thing he saw before his vision faded completely.

The time read 10:32.

Time Moves Forward

Max's eyes fluttered open, his chest rising with a deep, peaceful breath. The first thing he noticed was the gentle hum of the truck's engine, the soft glow of the world outside filling the cab with warmth. He blinked, his mind still heavy with the weight of what had just happened. For a moment, the world felt unreal—like he was caught between a dream and waking life. And then his gaze shifted to the dashboard.

It wasn't flashing anymore.

The clock read 10:33.

Time had moved forward.

Max exhaled slowly, his breath shaky but calm, as though the entire weight of the universe had just lifted off his chest. Something had shifted. The air was lighter, the space around him no longer pressing down with the suffocating weight of guilt and regret. He blinked again, trying to reconcile the strange calm he felt with the chaos that had just consumed his life.

He was no longer in the bank, no longer staring at that final moment of his life. His body wasn't on the cold floor, bleeding out, gasping for breath. No, he was here, in the truck, alive—and the world, the very fabric of it, seemed to pulse with a gentle, golden light. It was as though the air itself shimmered with possibility, like the sun was perpetually setting, casting long shadows that danced across the horizon.

Max let his gaze drift outside the truck. The world outside was almost surreal, bathed in a warmth that was unlike any sunset he had ever seen. The light was alive, breathing, almost as if it was embracing him, welcoming him into something new, something whole.

And then, in that stillness, Max heard a sound—a soft, melodic laugh. It was so faint at first, he thought it was in his imagination, but then it came again, clearer, richer, filled with a kind of joy that made his heart ache with longing.

His breath caught in his throat, his heart racing. He turned slowly, his pulse thundering in his ears.

In the backseat of the truck, nestled in a small car seat, was a baby. The child was perfect, small and delicate, with wide, curious eyes that sparkled with an innocence Max hadn't seen in so long. The baby's tiny fingers curled around the edges of a soft blanket, its chubby cheeks flushing with warmth as it laughed again—a sound that filled the space like music, wrapping around Max and filling every crack in his heart.

Max stared, his chest fluttered with a surge of emotion so strong, it almost knocked the breath from his lungs. His mind struggled to grasp what he was seeing, the sheer impossibility of it. The child looked at him, those bright eyes studying him with a quiet curiosity, and Max felt something inside him break open.

His lips trembled, his heart swelling with a love so intense it felt like it would consume him whole. This was real. The child was real.

He blinked, tears filling his eyes, and as they spilled over, he turned, his breath catching in his throat once more.

He turned, trying to grasp what was going on, there in the passenger seat beside him, was Eve.

She smiled at him, that same soft, knowing smile that had always made his world feel right, even in the darkest of times. Her eyes—those eyes that had once been filled with pain and exhaustion—now shone with a brightness he hadn't seen in so long. It was like looking at the sun after years of darkness, her presence lighting up every part of him that had once been broken.

"Max," she whispered, her voice like a gentle breeze, soft and familiar.

Max's chest fluttered, his throat closing up with emotion. He couldn't speak. He couldn't move. He could only look at her, his mind trying to process the miracle sitting right in front of him. Eve's hand reached out, her fingers brushing against his, and in that simple touch, Max felt everything—the years of love, the moments of heartbreak, the lifetime of promises that had bound them together.

Her skin was warm, real, and Max felt like he might shatter from the sheer force of the emotions surging through him. He had lost her. He had watched her slip away. And yet, here she was—alive, whole, more beautiful than he had ever remembered.

Tears slipped down his cheeks, his voice trembling as he finally found the strength to speak. "Eve…"

She squeezed his hand gently, her eyes shimmering with unshed tears of her own. "It's okay, Max. We're here."

Max swallowed hard, his gaze shifting back to the baby in the car seat. The child—their child—looked back at him with a smile so pure, so full of love, it was almost too much to bear. Max felt like his heart might burst from the enormity of it, the realization crashing over him in waves.

He turned back to Eve, his voice shaking. "How… how is this possible?"

Eve smiled softly, her eyes filled with love and understanding. "He's our son, Max. He's been with us this whole time."

Eve's voice softened, her eyes gleaming with tears as she glanced toward the baby, her expression filled with quiet gratitude.

"I've known for a while now," she whispered, her gaze tenderly lingering on the child. "He was with me too, Max. By my side, in the hospital. I felt him—his presence. At first, I thought it was just a comforting dream, but then…"

Her smile grew warmer as she looked back at the baby, a silent acknowledgment passing between them, as if offering thanks for the unspoken moments they had shared.

"There was one night… I was lying there, too weak to open my eyes, and I felt a hand. Small, warm. It rested on mine, just for a moment. Then I heard a voice—a whisper, like a quiet breath. It said, 'It's almost time.'" Her fingers gently brushed against the baby's cheek. "It was Eli. I didn't know it then, but I knew it was someone… someone we loved."

She turned her gaze back to Max, the deep emotion in her eyes reflecting the weight of everything unsaid.

"He was guiding me, Max, just like he's been guiding you. Guiding us through the darkness, Helping us both find our way back to each other."

Max's breath caught in his throat, the words sinking in like a revelation. The baby in the backseat—the one they had never been able to have, the life they had dreamed of but had never been given—was here.

Tears filled Max's eyes, and he turned back to the child, his heart overflowing with love and gratitude. He had spent so long grieving for the family they couldn't have, so long believing that he had failed Eve. But now, here, in this moment, he understood.

They hadn't failed. They had never failed.

Max reached out, his fingers brushing against the soft fabric of the baby's blanket, and as he did, the child's small hand reached up, grasping his finger with a strength that took Max's breath away. It was as if the child knew—had always known—the depth of their love, the way it had transcended time and space, the way it had always bound them together.

Max turned to Eve again, his voice barely a whisper. "I don't understand… how is this real?"

Eve's eyes shone with tears, but her smile never wavered. "Love, Max. It's always been about love. You gave me everything. You gave us everything."

Max blinked, the weight of her words sinking in. He had spent so long believing that he had failed, that he hadn't been enough. But now, sitting here with Eve and their son, he understood the truth.

He had always been enough.

Eve leaned in, her forehead resting gently against his, and Max closed his eyes, the warmth of her presence filling every part of him that had been cold and broken for so long.

"We're together now," she whispered, her voice soft and full of promise. "We have forever."

Max's chest tightened, his heart pounding in his ears. The world outside the truck seemed to shimmer, the golden light wrapping around them like a warm embrace. Everything felt alive, vibrant, and full of possibility.

And for the first time in what felt like forever, Max knew that they had everything they had ever wanted. They were whole—not because of the life they had imagined, but because of the love that had carried them through it all.

Max exhaled slowly, a deep sense of peace settling over him. He wasn't running anymore. He wasn't chasing after the past or trying to fix what couldn't be fixed. He was here, in this moment, with the two people he loved more than anything in the world.

And that was enough.

Max smiled, his fingers tightening around Eve's hand as he turned to look at their son one more time. The child—their child—laughed again, the sound filling the air like music, like hope.

The clock on the dash flickered one last time—10:33.

And in that moment, Max knew that time had moved forward. But more importantly, so had he.

The End

Thank you so much for reading my debut novel, The Cost of Forever. Your support means the world to me, and I would be incredibly grateful if you could leave an honest review at the site where you purchased the book. Your feedback helps other readers discover the story, and I truly appreciate every single one!

Acknowledgements

This book would not have been possible without the unwavering support, love, and encouragement from the people closest to me. To my family and friends, I offer my deepest gratitude for standing by me every step of the way.

First, to Cindy, my wife, my rock, and my greatest supporter. You have been my anchor through the storms of life, and without your belief in me, this journey would have been incomplete. Your love, patience, and encouragement gave me the strength to keep going, even on the hardest days.

To my family, thank you for always pushing me to chase my dreams, for your understanding every time I needed it, and for your endless supply of encouragement and advice. I am beyond grateful to have such an incredible family who has cheered me on from the beginning.

To my friends, your support has meant the world to me— whether it was offering feedback, listening to ideas, or simply asking how things were going. Every small gesture made a difference, and I could not have done this without each one of you.

Finally, to every person who believed in this story and helped bring it to life, from the biggest roles to the smallest—thank you. Your belief in me and this story has been a gift I will always treasure.

With gratitude,
John H. Adams